stop that wedding

MELISSA KLEIN

Rusty Wheels Media, LLC.
P.O. Box 1692
Rome, GA 30162

ISBN-13: 978-0692165096
ISBN-10: 0692165096

iii

To everyone who attempted to stop my wedding.

To everyone who wept as I walked down the aisle.

To everyone who said it would never last.

Love conquers all.

-Melissa

For projects past, and this precious book. Let there be many more in our future...

-Marc, RWM

Table of Contents

Diana Curtis stood behind the barricade at Jackson-Evers International Airport waiting to collect her mother from a vacation touring England's gardens. "Have you seen my mother?"

Mrs. Frasier, president of Greenville's Garden Club, waved and smiled. "No time to talk now, dear." The woman kicked it into high gear, sprinting past others also arriving at the Mississippi airport.

"Dang, I didn't know the old gal could walk that fast."

While others bore signs or flowers, to welcome their travelers home, Diana carried a roll of antacids in one hand and a cell phone in another. What was taking so long? All the passengers had cleared customs in Atlanta. She pressed a hand to her stomach. Her mother's last transmission before boarding her flight from London had sent her stomach churning and her anxiety pinging.

I have a surprise for you.

Coming from a typical mom, that message might mean a tin of shortbread biscuits or a Big Ben-shaped teapot. From Jackie Bouvier Dansfield Curtis it could mean any number of things. None of them good for Diana's ulcer or her bank account. Several more familiar ladies made their way past. All ignoring her query as they scurried off to baggage claim.

What is Mama dragging home this time?

Her phone vibrated in her palm. Turning her attention from the arrivals door, she prayed for another message from her mother. Instead she found a text from her head buyer.

No textiles in latest shipment. Only girl's accessories and toiletries.

Diana popped an antacid. Since starting the first Sweet Tea and Lavender store five years ago, she'd taken off exactly seven days. Five had been Christmases, one to have her wisdom teeth extracted, and another for her graduation from Ole Miss with a degree in business. Diana likened her string of boutique gift stores dotting the south to pearls worn by a sorority girl—breathtakingly beautiful, classic, and expensive. Her brainchild also required constant nurturing and attention. Just like her mother who dwelled in a fantasy world of garden parties and historical romance novels.

As long as the SEC merchandise arrived we're fine.

While Black Friday came for most retailers at Thanksgiving, hers arrived during the weeks leading up to the college football season.

She glanced up, worried she'd miss her mother. Jackie had the attention span of a drunk squirrel and was, therefore, prone to wander if something caught her fancy. Diana tossed the roll of antacids back in her purse and fished out the bottle of prescription anxiety medicine.

"Why didn't I take the time off and go with her like she asked?" Diana muttered, popping a pill. Clearly, that would have been the less panic attack-inducing solution.

Yet another lady from home walked past the roped off area. "Mrs. Beecham, a moment please."

The woman paused, sighed, and then doubled back.

Thank God for pastor's wives.

"Please tell me my mother didn't miss her flight."

The woman in her late sixties arranged her features into a smile. "She stopped off to freshen up. She'll be along in a while."

Diana let out a breath. "Thank heavens. I can't tell you how relieved I am to hear that. My imagination has cooked up all kinds of trouble my mother could get into."

"You're a good daughter to Jackie." Mrs. Beecham patted Diana's cheek before rejoining the line headed to baggage claim.

When several more work-related texts had her phone singing, Diana joined the travelers at the oval-shaped carousels. The sooner she got her mother dropped off at Greenbrier, the family's antebellum home forty miles west of Jackson, the sooner she could tackle the multiple work issues piling up. Besides her retail stores, Greenbrier's bed and breakfast accounts needed her attention and the hunters' camp she'd recently purchased required a visit.

After locating the correct carousel, she stood shoulder-to-shoulder with the crowd waiting for their bags. With summer travel season in full swing, the area had more people squeezed in it than a tailgate party at an Ole Miss game. A rotund man with a cart pushed his way forward to the front of the circular conveyer belt. His bull-in-a-china shop impersonation sent a young mom with two kids in tow bumping into Diana. In turn, she knocked against the person to her left.

"Excuse me." She turned to the man dressed in the nicest gray suit she'd ever seen. The finely woven fabric appeared hand crafted. Facing away from her, the gentleman didn't react to her entering his personal space, but good manners dictated she apologize nonetheless. "I'm terribly sorry."

Mr. Fancy Suit let out a growl. "Damn Yanks." The muttered oath shouldn't have gotten under her skin. His clipped British accent gave him away. *Bless his heart*. He didn't know many in her region of the US considered "Yankee" a curse rather than a national identifier.

"It's bloody bedlam in here. Don't these people know how to queue?"

A sharp retort poised on Diana's lips. She didn't complain about `driving on the wrong side of the road when she had traveled over there for business. Or the fact she couldn't get grits and ice tea. When in Rome, and all that. The sight of her mother's suitcase saved Mr.

Suit from the cutting down he so richly deserved. She wormed her way toward the revolving black belt.

Timing her snatch-and-grab, she captured the handle and pulled, only to be carried along when she failed to lift the heavy case off the carousel. People scrambled to get out of her way as she rounded the curve—all the while trotting backwards on her red-soled heels. *This is how I die!* She could imagine the *Greenville Post* headlines, "Former debutante killed in suitcase mishap. Closed casket required."

"Here, let me help you." In a fluid motion Mr. Suit wrapped an arm around Diana's waist and tugged her mom's bag free from the belt. He set them both upright and steady on the floor as if neither weighed more than a bag of sugar.

She blinked up at the guy who'd been so surly only moments before. "Thank you kindly. I do believe if you hadn't come along, I was facing certain dismemberment."

His smile sent her heart to sputtering, something it hadn't done since she caught her ex-boyfriend in bed with her ex-best friend. Contrary to popular humor, Brits had good teeth, especially the gentleman in his early thirties standing before her. Full lips perfectly accentuated his pearly whites.

"You're quite welcome." His hazel eyes sparked as if somehow, he found her amusing.

Ordinarily she would have taken offense at being the butt of someone's joke, but the flash of dimple on his left cheek made her want to say something else amusing. Instead she tugged on her mother's luggage. While the rest of the world carried bags with wheels, her mother clung to a matching set of Louis Vuitton passed down from Diana's grandmother, Bette. The case refused to budge, giving Diana a sudden flashback.

"Allow me." Mr. Suit hefted the case, removing them from the throng to the edge of the baggage claim area. "My God, woman, what did you do—steal the crown jewels?"

Diana smoothed the blonde strands that had come loose from the knot at her nape. "It's my mother's bag and it's entirely possible." At the very least Jackie had purchased replicas of famous jewels to add to her collection of all-things-British. She caught Mr. Suit's gaze and winked. "If she has your crown and scepter, I'll see to it you get it back." While clearly not one of the often-photographed members of the royal family, his smart appearance and manners certainly identified him as a member of Britain's upper echelon.

Why on earth was he slumming with the mundane multitudes?

Andrew had never wanted to kiss a stranger—until this moment. The woman he'd rescued from death-by-luggage elevated chatting up a chap to an art form. The snap of her green eyes conveyed intelligence while her ready smile hinted of sensual pleasure. Were all Americans this outgoing, or was it only this woman who'd ensnared him?

No wonder Uncle Neville had gotten into this mess.

"They're not my jewels per se," He winked. After all, at Eton he'd earned his reputation as a rounder for more than his card skills. "However, I do know the correct persons to whom you should return them. If you'll provide your contact information, I'll make certain of their safe return."

Her eyes narrowed. "I don't believe I caught your name."

Ah, wisdom behind that ready smile. "Andrew Montgomery." He left out the Viscount Farthingworth part. His title tended to attract the wrong sort, much like his uncle had as Duke of Effingham. Eventually, Andrew would bear both titles, adding to his eligibility as groom bait. "At your service. Miss?" He bowed ever slightly.

"Diana Curtis." She extended her hand, taking his in a firm grip. "What brings you to Mississippi? Business or pleasure?"

Her words snapped him out of his daze. He'd been so completely taken with the charming lady, he'd forgotten his purpose in flying to the States. Andrew glanced at the carousel for the black cases with the Effingham crest. "My uncle seems to have gotten himself in a spot of a situation. I came to sort him out."

Diana nodded. "I can identify with that problem." Her drawl threatened to distract him again. "My mother is the kindest, most generous person I know, but she has as much common sense as God gave a billy goat." She rubbed between her brows. "Mama lives in a fantasy world. Do you know she sent a birth announcement to the Prince and Princess of Wales when I was born?" All the while she told her story she scanned the throng of people, presumably looking for the flighty woman.

"Did their royal highnesses respond?" Where was his uncle? As much pleasure as he drew from chatting with Diana, he needed to straighten out the situation and return to Monte Carlo.

"Their note of congratulations was framed and has been in my bedroom since it arrived."

Something about Diana's candor—and her lovely heart-shaped face—enticed him to share his own parental woes. "Let me tell you what my Uncle Neville has done." Though his father, the Earl of Somerset, was still living, his maternal uncle was the guiding force in his life. To learn he'd behaved quite out of character, unsettled Andrew more than he was willing to admit. "It seems he's been corresponding with a woman from here in Mississippi. He invited her for a visit. Following a two-week courtship, he put my grandmother's ring on her finger, left a note with the butler, and headed here to meet her family."

Diana placed her hand on his arm. "It sounds as if we both have our hands full. The last message I received from my mother said she had a surprise for me." She held up a roll of antacids. "Surprises from Jackie are rarely pleasant, for me at least."

"Whatever your mother has done, I'm sure you'll be able to manage it. You seem like a woman who knows what she's about." He shook his head. "Me, on the other hand, I'm in for it. The butler, Cullen, described the woman in the ghastliest terms. He said she had hair as dark as a raven's wing and teased into something that looked like a nest for a large bird. To say nothing of her garish wardrobe. Usually,

I'm as egalitarian as the next chap, but this is beyond the pale. Mark my words, she's a gold digger." Not that her digging would do her any good. Still, duty demanded Andrew protect the retiring gentleman who spent more time in his library reading fifteenth-century literature than he did keeping up with twenty-first-century culture.

Andrew scanned the crowd, aiming his sights at shoulder height of the crowd. If only he could separate Uncle Neville from the clutches of this woman with a minimum of fuss. Drawing the stares of strangers ranked high on his to-be-avoided list. Just like romantic entanglements.

A fresh wave of anxiety washed over Diana. The knot in her stomach tightened to the point no amount of antacid could help. Andrew's description touched a little too close to home. Perhaps to outsiders, Jackie's bouffant was a little full. But her mother had always said, "The bigger the hair, the closer to Jesus."

You're borrowing trouble.

Lots of middle-aged women teased their hair and colored it a shade or two darker than they should. Besides, her mother's trip entailed tours of gardens, not ensnaring old men.

From several yards away, she caught a flash of fuchsia, her mother's signature color. Diana waved to catch her attention. "Yoo-hoo, Mama, over here."

Jackie weaved through and around people, smiling and waving all the way as she closed the distance. "I'm home, baby. Safe and

Sound."

Diana turned to Andrew, who'd finally located his uncle's luggage. "Maybe her surprise isn't so bad after all. She looks fine."

"Hey, sugar, let me hug your neck." She did and added a peck on the cheek. "You are a doll for picking us up."

"Us?" She squeaked out the word.

Her mother tugged a short, portly gentleman forward through the throng of people. "Diana, I'd like you to meet the Duke of Effingham, my—"

"Uncle Neville, what the bloody hell?" Andrew cut between the two lovebirds. "Have you lost your mind?"

Diana's head practically exploded as the pieces slid into place. Her mother patted her gentleman friend's balding head while the duke looked bashfully at his nephew—who'd called her mother a gold digger!

Balling up her fist like Granddaddy Dansfield taught her, she punched his jaw a good one. "You take what you said about my mama back, right this minute." She jabbed a finger toward the pair. "Whatever unholy mess these two have gotten into, I assure you my mother is not after your uncle's money or his stupid title." Thanks to Diana's drive and horse sense, money wasn't a problem for her family—anymore.

The crowd around them grew quiet, which was saying something considering they were in the middle of baggage claim. Her hand flew to her mouth. Good Lord, she'd assaulted a man. She could go to jail.

Pride flashed in Andrew's face for a moment, sending her heart into her stomach. Her grandmother always said, "a wound to a man's ego was as lethal as one to his chest." He rubbed the bright fist-shaped mark, moving his jaw. "My God, woman, are all American women versed in the pugilistic arts?"

"I'm so sorry. I don't know what came over me."

He motioned around the open area where people still observed their drama. "Is there a place we could discuss this matter in private? I'll be happy to render your mother an apology, but I'd rather not provide the masses with quite so much entertainment."

Andrew's steady tone did nothing to settle the buzzard flapping around in her belly. More than restoring her mama's honor needed attention. Jackie had been on the verge of declaring something regarding her relationship with the duke. Had she heard Andrew correctly? "I suppose the best place to do that is back home."

Jackie's hands flapped with excitement. "What a good idea, Diana. I can't wait for Neville to see where we'll be spending half the year."

Andrew opened his mouth, cut his gaze at her, and clamped his lips together.

"My car is in the parking deck. There should be room for everyone." If they didn't mind the extra "cargo" rolling around inside. While her office and bedroom were impeccably tidy, it seemed beyond Diana to maintain order in her vehicle.

"You'll love the gardens, especially the English cottage room I created a few years ago. The fairies and sprites find my hollyhocks and peonies delightful places to hide during the heat of the day."

Diana popped another antacid and rubbed the twitch forming above her right brow. She'd long ago given up wishing for a more conventional mother. "Jackie was as the good Lord intended," her grandmother always said. Since the age of twelve, Diana had taken care of her mother's day-to-day needs. However, as she looked over her shoulder at the two distinguished men Jackie had drug home, she couldn't help feeling this would be far more difficult than the time her mama brought home an injured deer. That fiasco ended when the buck ate the garden and gored the neighbor.

She cut her eyes at Andrew. Good Lord, he was a looker, even with a bruise forming on his jaw. This time she and her mother could both be in jeopardy.

Having procured a trolley for the cases, Andrew proceeded along behind the others. His plans for a quick return to his "occupation" slipped from his grasp as Diana and her mother discussed supper plans and accommodations for his uncle and him. It appeared they were on their way to the family's home where they'd sort out the mess in private.

As much as he loathed the situation, he had to give Diana credit for discretion—and the best rear view he'd seen in ages. Not only did her long ponytail draw attention to her narrow waist, those snug jeans were accentuating a perfect bottom. He shook away images of caressing any part of the scenery before him. His job was to extract Uncle from a certain middle-aged woman's claws, offer said woman an apology for derogatory remarks regarding her appearance and character and return them to their side of the pond.

Diana paused behind a mammoth white SUV. "Excuse the mess." She activated the rear gate to reveal a pink crate overflowing with tools, several towels, crumpled balls of paper, and a folding chair. "I wasn't expecting Mama would be bringing home quite so much extra baggage." She shoved the detritus to one side then reached for one of her mother's smaller cases.

Andrew stopped her. "Let me get the larger ones in first."

She scooted out of his way while he loaded the luggage puzzle in the back. With a little rearranging, he managed to make it work with enough room for the mother's carry-on. "I'll take that one from you now, if you please." As he reached back, their hands connected. He turned when she failed to let go. "What?"

"I'm so sorry." Diana touched his jaw. "Usually, I have better control over my temper."

Somehow, he didn't believe the statement, and as heat radiated from her touch he couldn't help imagining her temper and passion went hand-in-hand. "Think nothing of it." God knew he certainly needed to do the same.

"All right, then." She lowered the gate. "We're all set. Mama, why don't you join me up front?"

Jackie looped her arm through Uncle Neville's. "No thank you, sugar. Dukie and I want to sit together in the back, don't we, baby cakes?"

Diana's jaw tightened. "Don't you think—?"

"My minds made up, and I've counted to three." The woman stomped her foot.

"Fine." She let out a breath. "Andrew, looks like you're riding shotgun with me."

No wonder Mrs. Curtis had managed to worm her way into his uncle's life. She pouted her way through life like a spoiled child. As he climbed in the front passenger side seat, the farce got the better of him. "I think I'm going to be ill," he muttered. "Baby cakes? Dukie?" When had his uncle ever suffered such horrific familiarity?

Diana pointed to a takeaway bag crumpled in the floor. "There's a barf bag if you need it." She flashed a grin before starting the monstrosity's engine and driving them out of the car park.

Andrew shook his head at her jest. A bloke could learn to live on those smiles of hers. No! The situation in which he found himself was devoid of humor. After all, this woman could be leading them to their deaths. As they reached the motorway, thoughts of imprisonment flashed in his mind. What if they'd planned this all along? He and his uncle could be held for ransom, though their potential captors would gain little for their efforts.

He leaned his head against the headrest and vowed to keep his imagination in check. With enough real problems to fill the back of Diana's vehicle, he didn't need to create imaginary ones. His eyelids grew heavy. Prior to Cullen's call, he'd been "at work" for two solid days. A moment's rest would help him to see the problem better.

"The landscape is simply breathtaking, my dear. I can't wait to see it under spring's color."

His uncle's declaration penetrated his sleep. Andrew stretched and looked outside the 4x4's window at the farms and forests that lined the highway. "How long have I been asleep?"

"Fifteen minutes. We'll be at the house in another ten minutes or so."

Finally, they pulled into a long, stone drive bordered by ancient oaks on either side. Spanish moss hung from the limbs, providing a curtain to the road ahead. At a curve in the path, a classic example of Greek Revival architecture came into view. Two stories, symmetrical columns, wide porches on both levels. A newer extension peeked from one side, built in perfect sympathy to the original. Immaculately trimmed boxwoods and lush lawn greeted them as they approached the front of the home. Perhaps things weren't as bad as he thought if the Curtis women could afford such a mansion. His hopes popped like a balloon when they pulled around to the back and parked by the service entrance.

Diana killed the truck's engine and turned to her guests. "Welcome to Greenbrier, y'all." She tapped the horn, hoping one of the staff was nearby and could help with the luggage. Acquiring rooms for Andrew and his uncle ranked high on the current to-dos. Along with Googling their names. As they exited, her mother latched on to her beau like a sorority girl with a discounted Vera Bradley bag. Once she got her mother untangled from the duke, Diana could straighten the whole mess out.

Billy, a high schooler from down the road and the current bellhop, spilled out the kitchen door with Jasmine Doss on his heels. "Thank the heavenly angels." With her events manager on site, Diana could focus on her mother's current mess instead of the wedding taking place in their garden tomorrow afternoon. She tugged Jasmine to the side while Billy unpacked the back of her truck.

The African-American woman leaned in to whisper. "Did you know—?"

"No, and I don't have time to explain now. Please tell me we've got a couple rooms we can put these two gentlemen in." If push came to shove, they could stay in the family quarters, but the last thing she wanted was to give her mother an easy way for her and her British beau to cohabitate.

"The Azalea and Magnolia Suites are available tonight and tomorrow, but they're booked from Monday on."

"Not a problem. His Grace and his nephew won't be with us longer than that."

Jasmine's eyes bugged.

"You heard me."

"Man, when your mama…"

"I know. I'll fill you in later." She nodded to the couple. "First things first."

Inside the narrow hallway leading to the kitchen, Diana squeezed past the others. "I'll lead the way up to the front. We've got two nice suites for you gentlemen where you can freshen up and rest."

As they wound through the back offices, dining room, and library, her mother gave a commentary of the mansion's history, antiques, and noted visitors. To Diana, Greenbrier was more than genteel living. Returning home, even if she'd only been away a few hours, brought to mind the way her grandfather taught her to clean catfish, the scent of his cherry pipe tobacco, and her grandmother's famous biscuits. Which is why she needed to protect it and her mother—from all threats, foreign or domestic.

After arranging room keys and witnessing a kiss between lovers that turned Diana's stomach, she finally settled the British invaders in their rooms. As Diana and her mother walked the long way over to the mansion's 1920's addition where their rooms were, her mother kept glancing over her shoulder. "Do you think I should send up a tea tray? Neville loves his tea."

Diana let out a breath. She'd had enough of Dukie Dear and his sidekick. "If they want something, they can ring down to the front desk." She took her mother by the elbow. "Right now, you and I need to talk."

Her mother yawned. "Oh, darling, can't it keep? I'm knackered."

"Knackered? No, this can't wait. I need to know about this duke guy and how you two hooked up."

Jackie clutched her hands to her chest. "Oh, it's just too romantic." Her words came in with a girlish giggle. "The duke and I had been corresponding via one of my online gardening chat groups for a year or so before our trip. At first we discussed our mutual love of roses and peonies, but after a while, our conversations became more personal. When he learned the Greenville Gardening Club would be coming close to his home in Gloucester, he invited me to tea."

It all sounded innocent enough, except her mother had never shown any interest in dating. Not since Diana's daddy ran off with the town tramp. Swearing off men was about the only thing mother and daughter had in common. Diana too had put romance on a shelf after finding her boyfriend and best friend in bed together.

"That's very nice, Mama, but why did he follow you back here?"

"For the wedding, silly."

Diana choked on her own spit. "Say that again." Andrew had been correct. She glanced at her mother's left hand. Sure enough, there was a sizable ring on the third finger.

MELISSA KLEIN

"The duke asked me to marry him. We'll have the ceremony here in a couple weeks and then return to his estate for the rest of summer. The plan is to spend six months in each home, but we haven't worked out the details yet." Jackie wandered over to the window. "I think the knot garden will be the perfect place for the ceremony. Don't you?"

"You mean to tell me after one face-to-face meeting he proposed marriage?" My God, maybe the duke was crazy. Or more likely labored under the impression his American lady friend owned the mansion she lived in.

"He joined me and the ladies on the rest of our tour. We had a few days together before my trip ended, so it wasn't exactly on our first meeting."

"What do you know about this man?"

"I know he's the eighth Duke of Effingham, and his family has lived on his estate since the seventeenth century. He went to Oxford, loves Renaissance art, and is passionate about gardening. Most importantly, he's devoted to me." Her lip quivered with the last statement.

Diana wrapped an arm around her mother's shoulder. "It's all right. Don't cry. But you can't bring home random strangers and expect me not to react."

Her mother leaned into Diana's shoulder. "Can't you see we're perfect for each other?"

Only if fools came in matching sets—or every con had his

21

perfect mark. She had to find a way to expose the Duke of Effingham and his nephew—if that's who they were. "We'll talk more after you've had a rest, Mama." She pulled down the covers and helped her mother crawl atop her canopy bed.

After closing the door to her mother's room, Diana found herself too keyed up to turn in and too anxious to work. She left the new addition where the family lived and headed to the pool at the back of the mansion. After toeing out of her shoes and rolling up the hem of her jeans, she lowered her legs into the cool water. "Short of a crowbar, how am I going to pry those two lovebirds apart?"

"I've been contemplating that very thing myself."

The masculine voice from over in the corner made Diana jolt so hard she nearly toppled into the water. "What the hell. Do you always hide in dark corners?"

Andrew eased off the chaise and ambled over to join her at the pool's edge. "Not as a rule." He shrugged. "Then again, I don't usually have this kind of problem to navigate."

His nearness as he settled in next to her set the buzzards in her belly to flapping again. "Too bad we can't lock them in their rooms until they come to their senses." A smidgen of truth lay in her joke, along with a little reminder that she needed to keep her own hormones in check.

"Have you tried reasoning with your mother?"

Diana barked a laugh. "You met her right? The one in the fuchsia dress who brought home a man she barely knows. Logic and Jackie are not friends." Mama lived in a fantasy world filled with magical gardens, knights in shining armor, and happy endings. "How about your uncle? Is he prone to flights of fancy?"

"No, not at all." He shook his head, a puzzled look on his face. "I planned to speak with him, but he nodded off before I could get more than a couple sentences in." He sighed then scrubbed his palm over his face. "I'll try again in the morning when we're both fresher."

"I'm not feeling too sharp myself. I've been putting in long hours between the B&B, the stores, and the hunters' camp." The fancy new mattress she'd recently purchased called her name.

Andrew tugged on the dark golf shirt with the Greenbrier logo on the front. "I did a little shopping in the lobby boutique. From what the clerk tells me you've accomplished this all on your own and in a very short period. Well done."

Heat from his gaze warmed her. "Thanks." She looked away. "You're not the only one who's been nosey. I researched you and your uncle on the internet. Seems you two are legit."

"I assure you we are."

"But that's not all I learned."

He cocked an eyebrow. "Do tell?"

"I think I've got this straight. It's about as clear as the muddy Mississippi." Diana tapped her lips. "Since the duke doesn't have any kids, his title must go to the next closest male heir, which happened to be a distant cousin."

"A *very* distant cousin," Andrew added. "My family hasn't been very good at keeping our men alive."

Finding an heir wouldn't be a problem if they let women inherit. Only the good Lord knew who would have gotten their hands on Greenbrier if her Granddaddy couldn't have left it to her.

"Then, the duke's younger sister, your mama, married that *very* distant cousin which keeps everything nice and tidy."

"When the time comes, I'll inherit the dukedom as well as my father's titles."

"But you're Viscount Farthingworth now."

"Correct. See, that wasn't so hard to understand."

"The website didn't say what you do for a living, though."

"If you mean do I have a nine-to-five job, the answer is no."

"So viscounting is a full-time gig?"

"I have ways of keeping occupied."

She rolled her eyes. "I can well imagine." She met his type at Ole Miss. The accent might be different, but the attitude was the same. Another frat boy looking for a party.

The corner of his mouth turned up. "You're probably not far off the mark. Compared to you, my pursuits seem frivolous."

That smile. Those blue eyes of his. She looked down at her feet as they stirred the water. "Then why don't you change? You certainly seem smart enough to do something other than gallivant all over Europe. It wasn't like I was born running a store." Why was she talking about Sweet Tea and Lavender? To keep from thinking about how well he filled out his shirt, that's why.

"My pursuits serve a purpose. Enough about business." He pointed to the original 1832 house where the B&B guests stayed. "Tell me about *your* family and how *you* came to own such a beautiful specimen of Greek Revival architecture."

A spark of indignation flickered at the inference her people had somehow come by the house illegally. "My three times great-granddaddy won it in a poker game at the end of the Civil War. Him being a riverboat captain, he wasn't interested in farming, so he let folks in the area work the land in a lease-to-own type proposition. He gave the house and ten acres surrounding the place as a wedding present to his wife, a Creole woman he met down in New Orleans. You might say my people have never been high society even if we were stepping in high cotton."

His gaze danced in amusement. "And the present generation? What type of cotton are they stepping in?"

Was he poking fun at me?

Diana reined in her temper before it got the better of her. Again. She'd already proved nothing good came from letting this man get under her skin . "Medium height."

"What I meant was, do you have any siblings, extended family and the like?"

"I'm an only child of an only child." She drawled out the words, making them as sweet as her mama's ice tea. "My grandparents passed away a few years back, and Daddy left when I was in kindergarten." She had vague recollections of him—dark hair worn slicked back, bright green eyes, and a Corvette.

"Boyfriends?"

"Not anymore." She looked away. Thoughts of Travis and Megan locked in a heated clench still stung.

Andrew cupped her cheek, turning her to face him. "I sense I've touched on a tender subject. Forgive me."

That posh accent of his soothed over her like a velvet blanket. "Nothing to forgive. You didn't sleep with my best friend."

"What kind of fool would do such a thing? You're one of the most exquisite women I've ever met." He brushed back a lock of her hair. "You're smart, loyal to your mother…"

Her cheeks heated with his praise.

"And modest." He touched her cheek. "I've made you blush."

"I haven't heard this much praise since my granddaddy passed. You and your charming ways remind me a little of him."

"He would have liked me?"

"No, he would have hated you and your uncle on sight." She burst out laughing as his expression fell. "Don't be offended, though. No one was good enough for his girls."

"Your laugh does funny things to me."

"Ha, ha funny or funny like you're going to throw up?"

"No, like I want to do this." Andrew leaned in pressing his lips to hers. Then he drew her closer, angling her chin to deepen the kiss.

Diana kissed him back, threading her fingers through his hair. Man, did he know what to do with his lips and tongue. Parts as dormant as daffodils in December suddenly bloomed to life.

She broke the kiss, shoving him away. With the back of her hand, she wiped away the feeling of his mouth against hers. "No, no, no."

Andrew's eyes widened, and he scooted out of arm's reach. "I apologize. I would appreciate it if you'd refrain from slugging me again."

"No need to apologize, and I have no intentions of hitting you." Especially given how much she enjoyed the kiss. Her head hummed like she'd been hitting Phi Gamma Delta's bathtub gin. It was one thing to find Mr. Viscount Hotness attractive but letting the girly parts do the thinking was what got her involved with Travis Briscoe. Besides, she was supposed to be working on a plan to get rid of Dukie Dear, not making out with the younger version.

With absolutely no grace, she withdrew her legs from the pool and scrambled to her knees. "I gotta go."

"Wait." He reached for her. "We haven't—"

Panic set in. It was one thing for her mother to behave foolishly. It wasn't how she operated. One glance at Andrew's shocked and hurt expression and sticking around to explain wasn't a possibility. She needed a sure-fire reason to escape. "I'm about to pee my pants." The tacky comment lacked the good manners she'd been raised with, but it did the trick.

She caught Andrew's "by all means" comment as she fled through the bushes to her room. Future Diana would have to deal with the mess her mama dragged home from England because Present Diana wanted to resume kissing the hot viscount still standing by her pool.

The next morning, Andrew exited his room on the mansion's mezzanine level, taking a set of curving stairs to the lobby. Unaccustomed to keeping daytime hours, he shielded his eyes against the sunlight streaming in through the front door's beveled glass. The rays gave the space a warm, wholesome glow that vaguely irritated. He shook off the sensation and approached the check-in desk where the scent of gardenias greeted him along with a mid-thirties woman.

"Good morning, your lordship. Will you be joining His Grace for breakfast?"

"Momentarily. And please, Andrew will do."

Diana's already up and briefed her staff of peer etiquette. Would her conscientious nature also have her regretting their kiss? Did he? Giving in to impulses certainly wasn't his norm.

He noted the woman's name tag. "First, Debbie, I was

wondering when the gift shop might open." He tugged on the shirt he'd purchased last night. "It appears I'll need another change of clothes." Not that he planned to be here in the wilds of western Mississippi much longer, but he'd be damned if he'd fly back wearing the same set of clothes.

Debbie reached in a drawer for a set of keys. "At ten o'clock, but I'll be happy to open up now if you like. Anything you need to make your stay more comfortable, please let me know."

A large butterfly net for my uncle. "That's wonderful, but there's no need to trouble yourself. I'll come back after breakfast."

Andrew entered the breakfast room with its magnolia motif wallpaper and large cherry dining table and smiled when he found it empty save for his uncle. After pulling the French doors closed, he took the seat to Neville's right. "I'm glad to see you up. I trust you rested well and are thinking clearheaded this morning."

Uncle Neville dabbed the corner of his mouth with a linen napkin. "I'm feeling remarkably well considering the jet lag."

"Excellent." Andrew's stomach tightened. His uncle meant the world to him, and the last thing he wanted was to see him hurt by anyone—Andrew included. "I was hoping we could discuss your engagement to Mrs. Curtis."

"I'm sure you have concerns. Otherwise, you wouldn't have left Monte Carlo. I know more than you think I do." Uncle Neville turned to face Andrew. "As much as I find discussing money distasteful, I can assure you Mrs. Curtis isn't interested in our money."

But was Uncle Neville interested in hers?

An influx of cash would certainly help replace the ancient heating system at Chatham Park. To say nothing of what a few thousand pounds would do for the mansion's plumbing. Without the financial responsibilities of maintaining the estate, he might think of pursuing another profession. Despite what he'd told Diana, at one time Andrew had hoped to become a mathematics instructor. He excelled in the field of study and loved kids. In a perfect world, he'd already be married to the proper type of woman and well on his way to producing the heir and the spare. And the spare, spare.

Andrew brushed away the romantic notions and those concerning Diana's money. She'd worked hard to provide for her family, and he would continue to do the same despite his professional preferences. Thank God, his superior mathematical mind could also provide a way to earn large sums of cash to support Uncle Neville as well as his parents.

"What of Mrs. Curtis's past?" Diana mentioned her father was no longer *in situ*. Where was he now? Had there been other men?

"That seems rather old-fashioned."

"I'm only thinking of your best interest. You have a reputation to maintain."

"Jackie is free from any encumbrances precluding her from becoming my wife."

But was she? Diana hadn't mentioned a divorce—only that her father had run off. "So, you say, Uncle. However, you still haven't addressed the suitability issue."

"The people of Chatham will come to love her winsome ways just as I have."

An image of the St. Michael's Fete under her direction flashed to mind. "I beg to disagree with you, Uncle. However delightful you might find Mrs. Curtis, she's far from a suitable. Have you considered how she might cope with the duties of Duchess of Effingham?"

Neville waved away his concerns. "Minor details, minor details."

Before Andrew could refute his uncle's dismissal, the door opened, and the subject of their disagreement entered. With Diana close behind.

"Speaking of my lovely bride-to-be." Uncle Neville elbowed him. "On your feet, boy. You're in the presence of ladies."

Andrew rose and nodded to both women. "Good morning, Mrs. Curtis, Diana."

While Diana and her mother poured themselves coffee from the buffet, Uncle Neville leaned in to whisper. "Jackie has nothing but high praise for Diana. As beautiful as her namesake, a head for business, and a fiery temper to keep a man on his toes."

Andrew jerked his attention back to his uncle. Had the fairies made a body switch when he wasn't looking?

After pressing a kiss to Neville's cheek, Jackie took the seat to her fiancé's left. "I hope you both slept well. We have a lot to do today. So many plans to make. I can't wait for you to visit the springhouse."

Diana took a seat next to her mother and let out a deep sigh. So, she hadn't gotten any further with her mother than he had with Uncle Neville. Clearly it was going to take more than a conversation to get his grandmother's ring off Jackie's finger and his uncle on a plane headed east. The exact plan escaped him, but his gut told him it would take Diana's cooperation.

From the daggers she was shooting at him, she hadn't forgiven him for the kiss. The last thing he needed was for her to side with her mother and his uncle. "Mrs. Curtis, we started off badly yesterday." His gaze darted between Diana and her mother, hoping she'd understand the dual meaning behind the apology. "Please forgive me. I'm afraid my mouth got the better of me."

As Diana's cheeks flamed red, he extended a hand to Jackie. "I do hope we can be friends."

The woman's face exploded in a grin. "Of course, sugar."

"Apology accepted?" he pressed, waiting for a reaction from Diana. Her nearly imperceptible nod meant more than it should have.

"Most assuredly." Jackie patted his cheek. "I'm delighted you're here. This will give us time to get to know each other better before the wedding."

Andrew's stomach roiled at the thought. "About that, Diana, I was wondering if I could have a word."

She stood, and her phone played a jazzy tune. "Just a moment. This is my event manager's ringtone." She excused herself to the far side of the breakfast room before taking the call. Her frantic voice wafted back, cutting off the lovebirds' plans for the morning.

Soon, Diana returned to the table rubbing her temple.

Jackie turned toward her daughter. "What's wrong, baby? You look dreadful."

Diana pulled a roll of antacids from her pocket and popped one in her mouth. "That was Wes, Jasmine's husband," she said between chews. "The whole family has the stomach flu. She can't even get out of bed."

"How dreadful," Uncle Neville exclaimed. "And damned inconsiderate, if you ask me. I expect my staff to take better care with their health."

Jackie jumped up from her seat. "We should send over some chicken soup."

"Perhaps later, Mama." She tugged her mother back to her chair. "No one in the kitchen has time to make soup. Right now, I need to figure out what still needs tending to before the wedding guests start arriving."

"I know something that will help." Jackie extracted a silver tube from her pocket and handed it to Diana. "You should freshen up your lipstick. It'll make you feel better."

Diana clutched the tube like she might crush it. "Not now, Mama. I need to think. Surely there's someone who can pitch hit."

Andrew stood. "Perhaps I could be of assistance." A spark of hope flamed as a plan sprang to mind. Someone up there must like him because the situation couldn't be more advantageous for proving his point.

"How's that?" Diana cut her eyes at him. "Are you volunteering?"

"No, but if you'll walk outside with me, I think we can come up with a solution to several predicaments."

As they stepped onto the balcony, Diana noted her staff lining white chairs in front of a large arch at the back of the garden where the ceremony would take place. Nearer to the house, others were setting up small tables for the reception. She leaned over the railing to get a better look. Were those brown tablecloths? Not the color the bride had chosen.

She called down to the open expanse of lawn. "You guys hold up a minute before you set the tables." If only she could clone herself then she might possibly manage all the hats she needed to wear today. "What's your grand solution?"

"I propose you have your mother take charge."

Diana rolled her eyes. "Have you lost your mind?" He was supposed to be helping to fix this situation, not talking crazy. "She's not capable of organizing lunch for two, much less a wedding for one hundred."

"Exactly. I need to prove a point to my uncle. Our family has hosted the St. Michael's charitable fete since 1918. If he were to marry your mother, she would be responsible for organizing the event."

"Who does this now?"

"My mother, but as the Duchess of Effingham, it would become your mother's duty to maintain family standards. The fete is one of several social obligations. There's the Christmas open house and the annual garden show."

"Your plan is to embarrass my mother in front of her beau and potentially upset a wedding for your uncle to see sense? I won't have my mother humiliated." Her voice rose an octave.

He held his hands up. "Hear me out."

Unaware of her knee-jerk reaction, she unclenched her fist. "Fine, but this needs to be in the neighborhood of making sense."

"I imagine your event planner has already seen to the greater details of the wedding."

"I'm certain of it. Jasmine is as efficient as they come."

"What you require now is someone to take charge of the bridal party, make the guests feel welcome, and handle any situations that arise."

"Correct." Within her small circle of friends, Jackie could be quite gregarious and entertaining. However, decisions weren't her forte. Neither was dictating to anyone but Diana. Even their black lab, Buster, ignored Jackie's commands. "I don't see how it will work."

"My uncle is a stickler for protocol and family obligations. He takes his duty to the county and his role as duke seriously. If he feels your mother might not be able to cope, perhaps he'll reconsider this ill-conceived notion."

Diana let the idea roll around in her head. Between conference calls she could check in with her mother, and the staff would be doing most of the work. The possibility of Jackie's failure didn't set well, but then again neither did Jackie, Duchess of Effingham, taking on larger social engagements where folks weren't as understanding and the consequences for failure greater. In one of those rock-and-hard-place dilemmas, Diana made her choice. "It's a deal."

Andrew took the hand she offered. "It's settled then. You can set Jackie up with her tasks, and I'll direct Uncle Neville to a place where he can observe his fiancée in action."

Her stomach twisted for reasons other than a reaction to the flash of dimple when he smiled. "I don't like this at all."

His wide grin softened. "I understand, but we've got to be cruel to be kind. What they have is infatuation. I wouldn't give them more than six months before they were making each other miserable."

"I know." With another glance at the reception preparations be-low, she stepped toward the French door leading into the breakfast room. "There's an old southern saying, 'like must marry like.'"

Andrew followed. "Sounds reasonable." His hand went to the small of her back, sending licks of heat through her body. "Let's head back in and start breaking hearts."

Back inside, Diana squatted beside her mother. "Mama, Andrew has a solution for Jasmine's absence, but I need your help."

Jackie's blue eyes sparked. "Of course, baby. What can I do?"

Diana drew in a deep breath and prayed for forgiveness. "You take Jasmine's place today for the wedding."

Her mother's mouth formed an O. "I could never..." She grabbed Diana's hand.

It's for the best.

"There's no one else who can do it today. I have meetings I can't cancel, and everyone else has their own tasks to complete."

Twin furrows formed between Jackie's brows. "All I'd have to do is tell the wedding party when to walk down the aisle, right?"

Diana nodded. "You might also have to make sure everyone has enough food and drink."

A detail about the Williams-Perdue wedding popped in her brain. Jasmine said there'd been friction between the bride and her future mother-in-law. It was only fair Jackie had all the facts. Her inability to cope should conflict arise would simply prove Andrew's point. "And you know how feelings can get hurt at weddings. As event planner, it'll be your job to soothe any ruffled feathers."

"I don't know." Jackie chewed her lip.

The duke took Jackie's other hand. "Of course, you can help Diana. There's nothing to managing these types of things. It's simply a matter of being organized and keeping people's whistles wet."

Perhaps it was nothing if the hostess didn't tend to wander off to investigate a bird's call or begin discussing an obscure interest such as propagating geraniums. What if Jackie made a comment about the bride being in the family way?

Lord have mercy, her mama could ruin half of Greenbrier's business in an afternoon.

She opened her mouth to retract the offer.

"I'll do it." Jackie beamed. "If you think I can be of help, then I'll give it a try."

Diana stood on shaky legs. "You're a peach for helping me out. The guests should start arriving at eleven."

"Well, then I better find something appropriate to wear." Jackie gave the duke a peck on the cheek and drifted out of the breakfast room muttering, "I wonder if the bride would like to see my hydrangeas. They would make beautiful centerpieces. I'll be sure to find her when she arrives."

Panic gripped Diana. "If you gentlemen will excuse me, I have to speak to the staff."

"A word before you go." Andrew nodded toward the terrace.

Outside, she let her anxiety have free rein. "I don't like this one bit. We agreed my mother would not be humiliated."

Childhood memories flooded back. While the ladies in her gardening club understood Jackie and made allowances for her, that hadn't been the case with the parents of her classmates. More than once Diana overheard cruel comments regarding her family and their broken-down mansion. She'd been able to restore Greenbrier to its former beauty, but no amount of designer clothes could disguise her mother's limitations.

"You've made that clear, and I understand the desire to protect your mother. It's my motivation as well. However, I'm going to have to insist you not intercede. You must let the situation play out without your intervention."

"I have a conference call during the event I can't reschedule. There are also tax documents needing my attention, so I'll be in my office the whole time."

Andrew patted her arm. "Perhaps it's for the best. I'll let you know when it's over."

His kindness did little to sooth her anxiety. "Pray this works. Otherwise…" She left him to ponder what might happen if setting her mother up for failure didn't result in the duke breaking off the engagement.

Andrew stood open-mouthed like a carp as Diana stalked off, leaving her veiled threat behind her. The swish of her hair sent his train of thought into the ditch, especially as he imagined threading his fingers through it.

Beyond her beauty, he admired her loyalty to her mother. Jackie drove him to the brink of insanity, and he'd known her less than a day. Yet, Diana took her mother's idiosyncrasies in stride. What would it be like to share a life with someone as devoted as Diana? He slammed the door on the thought. Love was a luxury that pauper princes like Uncle Neville and he couldn't afford.

"Right. What was I doing?"

Neville's entrance onto the terrace brought Andrew's thoughts to the task at hand. "Uncle, we so rarely get to enjoy such fine weather. Shall we watch the festivities from here?" His scheme would work only if his uncle witnessed the debacle surely to come. He motioned for Neville to join him at one of the cushioned seats lining the flag-stone terrace.

"Capital idea. I can't wait to see my Jackie in action." He peered over the edge at the knot garden maze as if he expected her to spring from behind the shrubs. "She has quite a way with people, you know."

"So you keep saying." Andrew studied the ornate garden en-compassing nearly two acres. Divided into niches and herb-bordered sections, each area drew visitors in with a variety of plants. Even a non-gardener like himself could appreciate the amount of planning and work it took to execute such beauty. Jackie's real talent lay with flora not fauna.

While the wedding venue benefitted from enormous shade trees, the late morning sun bore down on them. By the noon wedding, he'd be as red as a tomato. He blew out his breath as a bee buzzed overhead. "I'd kill for a pint right about now." However, the ringside seat would serve the desired purpose.

Neville removed his straw hat and fanned himself. "Mad dogs and Englishmen, my boy."

A staff member he'd met previously approached from the stairs below. Rebecca set a tray on the table between them. "Miss Diana sent these over for your enjoyment."

"Thank you." He studied the plate of crust-less sandwiches and small appetizers. "Is this the wedding fare?"

"Yes, sir."

"That's all of it?"

Rebecca nodded. "With many newcomers moving in and marrying our folks, people now have sit-down receptions, but a good number still serve only light refreshments after the ceremony."

Uncle Neville raised a small cup of bright red liquid. "What in God's name is this concoction?"

"Raspberry punch, a long-standing favorite made with sherbet and Sprite."

"No alcohol." Uncle Neville's surprise matched his own. How did one properly celebrate a nuptial without at least a little champagne?

The server shook her head. "There won't be any alcohol at this wedding—nor dancing either. Not when the bride's family is among the founding members of First Baptist Church."

"It should be over and done with by tea time at that rate."

"Two hours tops start to finish." Rebecca pointed to the glasses of punch. "Give it a taste and tell me what you think."

Andrew took a tentative sip and got exactly as his eyes predicted. The sugary liquid coated his throat, and the half-melted sherbet did nothing to quench his thirst. "God, that's awful."

Uncle Neville sputtered. "That can't possibly be Greenbrier's signature drink. It's more likely to put Diana out of business."

Rebecca grinned. "I couldn't agree with you more, Your Grace. Our signature nonalcoholic drink is a refreshing sparkling lemonade I'll happily bring you."

"Sounds lovely," Andrew said, though he still craved a good ale.

Rebecca was quick in bringing the promised lemonade, and after one sip, he had to admit it did an excellent job of helping him forget the humidity.

"Speaking of lovely, there's my exotic bird."

Jackie entered the garden from the gate leading to the family quarters. However, instead of making a beeline to the early arriving guests, she trotted toward the arbor at the back of the garden where the ceremony would take place. Dressed in canary yellow, she stood out among the subtle green and ivory of the shade garden. It made for ease in watching as she flitted around the space, adjusting the floral arrangements. However, she should have been attending to her duties.

Case in point, a young couple who'd wandered the garden for several minutes approached Andrew and Neville. "Could you tell me where to place the gifts?"

"Just a moment. Let me find the event coordinator." Andrew scanned the garden for Jackie. Where had she disappeared to? "Uncle, do you see her?"

Neville leaned over the railing. "I'm not sure…"

"As duchess she can't—"

"There she is!" Neville gestured triumphantly to a stand of hydrangeas. "That lovely woman in yellow can assist you."

After the couple left, while Neville kept up a one-sided conversation about Jackie's gardening skills, Andrew waited for the woman's next *faux pas*.

Shortly, the bride exited the mansion, an entourage of female attendants and a photographer in tow.

"I want to get a few shots under the trees while the light is right." He pointed toward two oaks providing canopy for a stand of thick shrubs. "I'll get you back inside before your groom sees you."

The presence of the bride caught Jackie's attention, and she trotted on high heels over to the party. Rather than offering help, or simply observing, she interrupted the photographer several times, tugging on the guy's sleeve or standing between him and the bride. Finally, the photographer extracted something from his bag and handed it to Jackie.

Andrew cut his eyes at his uncle to make sure Neville was absorbing Jackie's behavior. If she became the Duchess of Effingham—God forbid—she would be the most senior woman in the county, social speaking. However, that didn't mean she could intrude or be overbearing. Quite the contrary, a true duchess didn't need to exert her position.

When Andrew looked back, Jackie had wandered away from the bride and was making a circuit from a table where the guests could sign a large picture frame, over to the gift table, and then to the caterers who were setting up for the reception. There, a conversation took place between her and a woman pouring bottles of red liquid into a punch bowl. The server handed Jackie a large tumbler of the vile punch, and she walked to the next station.

In the meantime, Uncle Neville had ceased his running

compliments. Even as love struck as he was, the man had to see Jackie was rubbish at organizing the event. The ceremony would begin in thirty minutes, guests were roaming the property, the caterers were off schedule, and Jackie was—chatting with the flower girl.

Bloody hell, his plan simply had to work. There was no way this woman could be the next duchess.

A sob from below the terrace caught his attention. "I can't believe Tommy's mother would do that."

Andrew leaned forward to see the bride and her mother. "I told you Delores Perdue is off her rocker." Dressed in a subtle shade of blue, the fortyish woman pointed several yards away to another middle-aged matron.

"Is she really dressed like that?" Uncle Neville asked, giving voice to his own question. The large woman had squeezed herself into a strapless ball gown—in the purest white imaginable. She even wore a short veil.

"What am I going to do?" The bride stretched the final syllable of her query into a whine that pierced his eardrum. "I'm the only one who's supposed to be in white."

"You'd think she would know that. But you know what I always say, breeding will tell."

The bride stomped her foot. "Well, Mother, being right all the time isn't helping us out of this situation, now is it?"

"Short of ripping the thing off her, I don't know what we can do."

The bride's tears began in earnest, giving Andrew a twinge of guilt for eavesdropping on the family's private moment. He and Neville exchanged a glance. "Perhaps we should—"

"Just a moment." His uncle nodded toward Jackie as she headed to the bride and her mother.

"Oh, dear. Tears on your wedding day won't do." If Jackie's hands flapped any harder, the woman would be in danger of taking flight. "Mrs. Williams, is there something I can do to help?"

The mother shook her head. "I'm afraid not."

"Tommy's mama is having trouble letting her only boy go."

"It didn't help we turned down her offer to have the wedding in her pasture."

"And I didn't want to use those ugly ole glasses she bought for the toasts, so her way of getting back at me is to wear that dress."

Jackie tapped a finger to her lips. "Don't worry about a thing. You two head back to the bride's room, and I'll have a little talk with your future mother-in-law."

The bride and her mother paused as if they were as skeptical as Andrew. In the end, they did as Jackie suggested and returned inside. Then she jumped into action, waving down the anti-bride with her red cup. "Yoo-hoo, Mrs. Perdue. I need a moment of your time."

Andrew held his breath. How could a woman with absolutely no tact defuse a situation already fraught with animosity?

Jackie tottered over, her pencil skirt and high heels inhibiting her walk. As she drew near, she stumbled, and for a moment she almost righted herself. With her next step, her heel caught in the grass and sent her colliding into Mrs. Perdue. Witnesses gasped, only to have their cries drowned by a bellow likened to an angry animal. When Jackie darted out of reach of the angry woman's flailing arms, the reason for the shouts became as evident as the splash of red down the front of the woman's white dress.

"Bloody Hell!"

The chorus and refrain of curse and apology lead the way ahead as the two women neared the mansion. "I can't apologize enough, Mrs. Perdue." Jackie repeated the mantra as they climbed the stairs to the terrace.

"You certainly can't." She shook her finger at Jackie. "Mark my word, I'll see to it no one in this town uses Greenbrier for so much as a dog show."

Andrew cringed. Talk about unintended consequences.

"If you'll allow me to make amends." Jackie's hands flapped in earnest. "On a recent trip to Europe, I purchased a beautiful dress perfect for this occasion. I believe you and I are the same size. I'd like to make a gift of it if you'll allow me."

Mrs. Perdue eyes widened. "What kind of dress?"

"A coat dress in the perfect shade of robin's egg blue." A mischievous grin turned up the corners of Jackie's mouth. "Alexander McQueen. I bet the bride isn't wearing couture."

"She's not. It's off the rack."

"Right this way then. You have just enough time to change

before the wedding starts." Jackie winked at Andrew and Neville as she passed.

Diana chewed her last antacid as Andrew finished retelling how Jackie baptized Greenville's PTA president with red punch. "Kill me now and bury the body. That'll save the lawyers the trouble of picking my bones clean."

"I'm truly sorry. I had no idea this would happen."

"How could you? Few know the inner workings of Jackie's mind." The throbbing in her own head had little to do with the accounting she'd done on Sweet Tea and Lavender's books. "I have a feeling you're not telling me everything. What else happened? Did my mother throw cake or open the wedding gifts?"

"Nothing as bad as that. She was just...unorganized." Andrew stood from the chair across from Diana's desk and paced the area between her desk and the window overlooking the pool. "During the ceremony the bridesmaids weren't spaced evenly, and your mum failed to signal the string quartette to play the processional."

What a goat rope.

If word got out, Greenbrier's business could be seriously impacted. "In other words, she proved your point."

"Exactly."

"Did your uncle notice?"

"Jackie's antics were rather difficult to miss. As soon as the last guest left, he excused himself to have a private word with her."

Being right should have come with a little more job satisfaction. "It's still early enough in the day you might catch a flight back home. I can have someone drive you and the duke to the airport if you like."

Andrew nodded. "That's most generous of you considering."

"It's not your fault. I should be thanking you. Your planned worked." With him leaving, telling Andrew the truth cost her nothing. "Under different circumstances, I could see us becoming friends. Aristocratic playboy or not, you're good people, Andrew Montgomery." *And definitely easy on the eyes.* "For the record, I want to apologize again for slugging you at the airport yesterday. But, I'm not sorry you kissed me. It's been a long time since I've played tonsil hockey, and it was quite nice."

"Right." He ducked his chin. "I should check on my uncle. I'm sure he's anxious to depart."

Diana joined him at her office door. "I'll follow you downstairs. I'm not sure where my mother will go to lick her wounds, but I imagine she'll want company." They walked in silence until they reached the kitchen. "I guess this is goodbye." She extended her hand. "I would say it was a pleasure meeting you—"

"But that's not exactly the right sentiment, is it?" His blue eyes sparked. "Shall we say it's been an adventure?"

"One neither of us will soon forget."

He leaned in, brushing her cheek with his lips. "Never in a million years."

Diana's heart leapt and sputtered as she turned away from Andrew. Why couldn't they have met on a beach somewhere? Not that she ever took vacation—but still. She would have enjoyed spending a few quiet hours getting to know Viscount Farthingworth a little better.

Nearing the family's private sitting room, Diana caught her mother's voice, pitched high with emotion. She slowed, girding her loins for the task ahead. Comforting Jackie in her heartbreak would be a Herculean task. She cracked the door and peeked inside. "Mama, how you doing, sweetheart?"

"I'm fine as frog's hair." Jackie bolted from the sofa to drag Diana into the room.

"Hello, my dear." Neville saluted her with his tea cup. "We're celebrating your mother's success. She was brilliant. The bride couldn't stop gushing, and the troublesome mother-in-law seemed happy enough in the end."

Jackie cozied up next to the duke. "We've also settled on a date for the wedding—one week from today."

A few hours after discovering Diana wasn't bidding goodbye to Viscount Farthingworth, she sat across from him at the supper table. She chased peas around her plate, wishing she'd skipped the emotional farewell and kept her admission inside her head where it belonged. Keeping her head down, she studiously avoided eye contact with Andrew. Sitting across from the man you'd bared your soul to wasn't awkward *at all*.

Her mother broke the silence. "Diana, darling, what time tomorrow can you go with me to look at wedding dresses?"

A mental image of playing Say-Yes-to-the-Dress with her mama popped into her mind. What if Jackie wanted a southern belle gown? Or worse, a mermaid style dress like Mrs. Perdue had! Diana rubbed the twitch above her right eye.

Well, at least she wasn't fixated on Andrew anymore. Thank the good Lord above, she also had the perfect solution to all her problems—a rare win, win, win situation. "I'm not free, and neither are you. Remember we'd planned to ride out to the hunters' camp tomorrow. We've been planning it for weeks. I've taken off work and everything." Sweet Tea and Lavender had been getting the short end of the stick in recent days, but as soon as she got rid of their visitors, she'd be able to devote one hundred percent of her attention to her first born.

Jackie's hands shot to her mouth. "I'd completely forgotten." She giggled. "I suppose I've had other things on my mind."

Andrew caught Diana's gaze. "You ladies should go ahead with your plans. Uncle Neville and I can keep ourselves occupied. You know what they say, 'absence makes the heart grow fonder.'"

"Nooo," Jackie morphed into full-on pout. "It's an overnight trip, and I don't want to be away from my sweetheart that long."

"I have an idea." Andrew's plan to prove Jackie's unfitness for her new position wasn't wholly flawed. It simply needed a different focus. "Neville, why don't you and Andrew join us? You need to see what you're in for if you're going to spend half your time here."

Neville dabbed the corner of his mouth. "Brilliant idea. In my younger days, I was quite sporty. Cricket, polo…"

This was too easy. No way these fancy boys could handle the backcountry. She turned to Andrew. "Do you enjoy country pursuits?"

"Contrary to popular belief, not everyone in Britain hunts and shoots." He arched an eyebrow. "However, as it so happens, I'm passable in the saddle."

"Good enough for our purposes. After dinner, I'll get your sizes, and have one of my staff get the gear you'll need from my shop downstairs. We'll leave bright and early in the morning."

"Yay," Jackie clapped her hands. "You're going to have so much fun at the camp. I can't wait to cook for you, Neville, darling. Food cooked over a wood-burning stove always tastes better to me."

"To say nothing of the well water. There's nothing sweeter." Andrew needed to know what he was in for. Plus, she enjoyed the way he shifted in his chair.

"You're saying there're no amenities where we're going?" He paled beneath the sunburn he'd caught earlier.

"That depends." Diana drew perverse pleasure from his discomfort. "I happen to think the sounds of nature outside my window at night and zero bars on my cell phone an amenity."

Neville jabbed his nephew in the side. "Where's your adventurous spirit, my boy? How bad could it possibly be?"

"I guess we'll be sleeping rough tomorrow night."

"It's not as bad as that," Diana said, lest he attempt to back out in the morning. She wanted Andrew to enjoy the full hunters' cabin experience along with his uncle. "The old homestead is fairly solid, and there are bunks in the cabin, so think more pre-Industrial Revolution than prehistoric."

His gaze darted to the others before settling on hers. "Cold comfort." He offered a weak smile. "But like my uncle said, how bad can it be—especially if you ladies can manage?"

Heat flared in Diana's belly, adding fuel to her fully involved irritation with the viscount. Did he assume nature had imbued him with untapped outdoorsman skills by virtue of his *appendage?* "Then you can wipe that scared-rabbit look off your face, can't you?"

She ignored her mother's shocked gasp, tossed her napkin onto the table, and headed to the door. "I'm going to the barn."

Diana stalked all the way to the back of the property. How did Andrew Montgomery manage to get her hackles up with so few words? She shoved the barn doors open and stepped inside. The scent of warm hay and motor oil tingled her nose. This had been her grandfather's domain, and entering his space was as close to a visit she'd get this side of heaven.

Oh, Granddaddy. You'd know what to say to calm me down—and get those damned Brits off my property.

"You look ready to spit nails."

She drew up short. "Hey, Doc James, I didn't expect to see you here this time of night."

"Hanging out with Sergeant for a while." He patted his quarter horse's rump. "I'd hoped to get a ride in, but I got held up at Jasper Dairy." He pointed to Diana. "Given your outfit, I'd say you weren't getting ready to take Jezebel out for a ride."

She looked down at the sundress Jackie insisted she wear to dinner. Flecks of mud dotted the pink fabric. "Jeez, I need to load gear into the truck, but I'd rather have a root canal than go back up to the house."

He continued brushing the gelding. "The rumors are true." James Bentley kept to himself and was known to prefer the company of animals over people.

After the past couple days, she could understand why. "Good Lord, if you've heard about Mama's fiancé, then it must be all over the whole county."

Her mother had tried fixing the two of them up way back in high school. The county's most popular veterinarian was certainly handsome enough to catch her eye. He'd also demonstrated time and again he had more patience than Jesus, Job, and her favorite lab, Buster, so Jackie wouldn't drive him insane. However, there were reasons James avoided most folks, darn good ones, she imagined. And that was enough to steer her away.

"You'd be surprised what folks insist on telling me. Miss Ruth told me when I went to see 'bout her coon dog."

Diana opened one of the unused stalls and began rummaging around for the equipment they'd need at the cabin. "I need a couple cast iron skillets, blankets, my water filtration system…"

Used as a hunters' cabin by the previous owners, the place already had a few pieces of furniture and a cook stove. They'd need to pack everything for the visit and things to leave behind for the next time. Eventually, she planned to outfit the cabin as a remote getaway for more adventurous guests. However, now she prayed it would suffice to show her mama Neville Montgomery wasn't cut out for true country life.

Doc James took the old-fashioned coffee pot from her. "Here, let me give you a hand."

"Thanks, doc."

"Should I hook the horse trailer to your truck for you?"

Taking the horses would be more fun. She and her mother loved riding the trails surrounding the town that led out to the country. Enjoyment wasn't tomorrow's objective. "Not the horse trailer, but you can help me hook up the other equipment."

Andrew thrummed his fingers against his thigh. The moment Jackie set her coffee cup back on its saucer and dabbed her lips, he pounced. "Lovely dinner, Mrs. Curtis. Southern cuisine certainly lives up to its reputation. Okra is indeed a delicacy, and your garden-fresh tomatoes tasted of the summer sun."

Jackie beamed with his praise. If only he could manage to say the right things to Diana. He looked beyond the dining room windows, to the rolling pasture and the barn at the far end. "If you'll excuse me, I have things needing my attention."

As he picked his way across the field, avoiding landmines and the cows that made them, he took a moment to appreciate the remains of the day. An earlier shower had cooled things off, and the nocturnal insects were tuning up for their evening chorus. In the shadows created by the giant oaks in the formal gardens, fireflies conducted a mating ritual that slowed his steps. He imagined holding Diana in his arms as they, too, danced. She'd be ethereal in evening wear, with her hair up and jewels at her neck.

Andrew slammed the door on the scenario. "Not going to happen." Certainly not considering her demeanor toward him at dinner. Not that he wanted to pursue a romance with her. "It's simply the scenery muddling my thinking. And jet lag. That's it." He increased his pace, determined to discuss Diana's plans for his uncle. Nothing more. Voices led him to the far side of the barn.

His brain skidded to a halt as he approached the gravel area where he found Diana leaning over the side of a battered truck. Sunlight reflected off her hair, turning it golden. As she extended her arms to place something in the truck's bed, the muscles on her bare shoulders flexed in sinewy beauty. His gaze slid south to the hem of her dress as it rode higher up her thigh.

A man dressed in worn jeans, boots, and a ball cap joined Diana by the truck. He hefted two large plastic containers into the truck bed. "Once I load the extra fuel cans, you should be all packed."

Diana slipped her arm around the man. "Are you sure I can't talk you into coming with. I'll make you my famous skillet peach pie."

He laughed and ruffled her hair. "Sorry, I'll have to take a pass this time. I've got too much work to do to take time off. Otherwise I'd be all over your offer."

From appearances, the guy would also be all over Diana given half a chance. The prospect sent a fissure of irritation through Andrew.

"I came out here to offer my assistance, but I see you already have a cavalier."

Diana jerked around. "What? No. I mean, yes. We're good. You can go back to the house. Wouldn't want you to miss your cigars and cognac." Her lips spread in a grin. "Like you said earlier, 'if I can manage, how hard can it be?'"

He cringed as she repeated his words. The sentiment he expressed didn't hold with his belief about women's abilities. It had simply been another example of Diana bringing out the stupid in him. "Um…" If only he could get his brain and mouth to work in unison.

Thankfully, Diana's friend offered a rescue. "James Bentley." He dusted his hand against his thigh before extending it to Andrew. "Local veterinarian and a long-time friend of Diana's."

"Andrew Montgomery, occupation questionable and recent acquaintance of Miss Curtis."

"You left out Viscount Farthingworth and heir presumptive to the Effingham dukedom," Diana added.

With good reason.

James' narrow-eyed reaction typified one of two ways people responded to learning of his peerage. Hungry excitement being the other.

"Those titles and five dollars will buy me a cup of coffee here in America. Call me Montgomery or Andrew if you like."

Suspicion cleared from the vet's face. "Will do, Andy. You and your uncle are in for a treat tomorrow. I've hunted and fished that land all my life. It's God's country." He turned to Diana. "Remember what I said about that sow."

"I hear you. I'm not anxious to tangle with a mama bear. I'll be packing my .45 along with my Benelli, just in case. But only as a last resort. I know how you feel about animals, domestic and wild."

Bears?! He and Uncle Neville were being led into a wilderness filled with marauding beasts. All in the name of love. If the prospect of facing death wasn't enough to convince his uncle he wasn't cut out for life as a southern gentleman, Andrew would have to concede defeat.

James tipped his hat. "I'll be off then. Nice to meet you, Andy. Enjoy your trip."

A smile crossed the man's face as he left, but Andrew gave over pondering the reason for more pressing matters. "Are we all set for tomorrow?"

Diana secured a tarp over the provisions in the truck bed. "Everything except last-minute food items. I had the clothes and boots you'll need sent to your rooms already."

Testament to how involved he'd been with the exchange between Diana and James, he'd failed to note the trailer attached to her truck until now. "I thought we were riding horses."

"I'm sorry if I gave you that impression." She patted one of the vehicle's seats. "No, we're taking the ATVs."

How hard could it be? It would be like riding a motorized, four-wheeled bicycle. Except. "There're only two of them."

"Look at you using math." She nodded, a smug grin creasing her face. "And you said you didn't have any marketable skills."

Andrew let out a growl of frustration. "Did I do something to offend you?" His words at dinner came to mind. "Other than insulting your capabilities earlier. For which I heartily apologize. But you were testy with me before I cocked things up."

Diana ducked her chin. "I'm embarrassed by what I said yesterday. I thought I wasn't ever going to see you again, otherwise I would never have said those things."

He drew near, unable to resist the lovely blush to her cheeks. "I'm awfully glad you did." He brushed her face with the back of his hand. "Remember, we're on the same side."

"We are, aren't we?" Her smile lit up his chest.

"Friends again?"

"Sure."

"What's your brilliant plan?"

She shrugged. "Make your uncle miserable."

And Andrew as well by proximity. "That's it?"

"Mama loves the outdoors, not just her neat-and-tidy garden, but the back country as well. She could never be happy with someone who didn't love camping and fishing as much as she does. You saw the pouting she did at dinner. She's going to expect Neville to accompany her on these trips."

"All right. I'll follow your lead." He held up a finger. "However, as you did with your mother, I must insist on parameters."

"Go for it."

God only knew what other hazards lay ahead of them. Diana must consider Neville's inexperience. "My uncle may not be placed in any grave danger. Bruises to his ego are a concession I have to accept, but I won't have his safety threatened."

"I can't make that promise." Her voice rose in surprise. "You heard James. There are bears out there, along with coyotes and snakes. Maybe a wild boar or two. I will tell you, your uncle won't be in any more danger than Mama or I am—or you for that matter."

The next twenty-four hours were guaranteed to be pure unadulterated hell. "To say nothing of the man-eating mosquitoes." He slapped at one of the insects that had landed on his arm and begun to draw blood. His sixth sense tingled, urging him to fold his cards, take his chips and run. However, caution hadn't made him the money to keep Chatham Park in family hands. Only something extreme would work. "I'll see you at first light then."

The morning star and crescent moon greeted Diana as she tramped across the wet grass to the barn. Finding Andrew waiting by the truck, she passed him a travel mug of coffee and a biscuit. "Operation Off Road Breakup is officially underway."

She pealed back the foil on her own breakfast and breathed in the spicy scent of sausage. "Go ahead. They're better while they're hot." Although stone-cold, her mother's biscuits were still something worth savoring. Diana followed up the first bite with a long draw of strong coffee. Fortified with carbs, fat, and caffeine, she might possible survive a morning of proximity with Andrew. Darn it all, for a slice of upper crust, he sure wore jeans and plaid well.

He moaned as he bit into the sausage biscuit. "Don't let my uncle..." Between chews he continued. "Neville can't have one of these or our plans are doomed."

"Good?"

He nodded, taking another bite.

"Don't worry. The first leg of our off-road journey will be enough to wipe all pleasant memories from his mind."

He swallowed then took a sip of coffee. "That bad?"

"I'm assuming your uncle doesn't enjoy a good bog wallow." The property she'd purchased bordered the state highway, with the acreage visible from the road devoted to quail hunting. Where they were headed, white-tailed deer and bass from a large lake were the quarry. Separating the two areas was a wide stream, damp even in the driest conditions. With rain falling nearly every afternoon, they'd be crossing at least a hundred yards of heavy mud.

"I don't know what that is, but I can assure you he does not. Neither do I."

"You'll see soon enough."

"Best to get started." He drew in a breath. "The sooner we begin this trial by nature, the sooner I can have a martini glass in my hand."

Diana's heart twisted. She'd miss Andrew once he and the duke were back where they belonged. It was unreasonable to have formed an attachment to him in such a short period of time, but losing her boyfriend and bestie had robbed Diana of her core of friends. "My mother popped back in for one more civilized potty break. Once she and your uncle get out here, we can get this show on the road."

Andrew's hang-dog expression tickled her. "At least you have the luxury of standing up. Mama and I—"

The appearance of her mother and Neville cut off the rest of her explanation. No doubt to Andrew's great relief, going by the florid color on his face. "Let's hurry, Mama. I hear the fish calling your name." For once Jackie wore clothes suited for the occasion and in muted tones. Unlike her fiancé who exited right behind his betrothed.

"Bloody hell." Andrew took a couple steps toward his uncle and narrowed his eyes.

"I couldn't have said it better myself." In place of the sensible Carhartt pants and boots she'd sent up to his room, the man had some-how gotten ahold of a cowboy outfit—from a 1950s' Western movie.

"That hat."

"I can get you one if you like." She carried a small line of western gear in the Sweet Tea and Lavender shop in the mansion's lobby.

He barked a laugh. "I'm good. At least with the red shirt you won't have to worry about losing him."

"True." Her mind wandered at the thought of her shop. For much of the trip, cell service would be spotty at best. "I'm going to check my emails one more time before we get going."

He waved her off. "Go ahead. I'll get these two sorted, and we'll be ready to start when you're done."

Diana pulled up her emails on her phone, scanning through the score of unopened messages for any urgent notes. After sending a quick reminder to the store manager in Anniston about an upcoming festival they were supporting, she checked the battery life. Ninety-eight percent would hold her for most of the day, and with an additional power booster, she'd be good to go.

Why did her stomach ache like she was abandoning a newborn puppy? "This must be how moms feel leaving their kids at kindergarten." She returned to the truck to find Andrew in front and the lovebirds occupying the old truck's rear jump seat.

"They insisted," he said as she climbed inside.

She started the truck's engine. "We might as well start as we mean to go on, Neville. I'm sure my mother warned you, that you're in for a rough ride out to the property."

He clutched his ten-gallon hat to his chest. "I'm sure I'll manage, my dear. Onward ho, and all that."

Diana couldn't meet her mother's beaming face for fear she'd burst out laughing. Their drive to the hunters' camp began with only the whine of tires against pavement for noise. The sun eased up over the trees bringing with it the promise of another beautiful delta day. About two miles in, Neville began using his hat as a fan.

She rolled down the truck's window to get a breeze blowing. "That should get some air moving." At the crest of a hill the turn off came into view. Turning right, she pulled into the gravel drive and stopped in front of a large metal gate.

Andrew popped the door handle. "I'll get that for you." He climbed out and did the honors, dragging the gate back into place once the trailer cleared. Afterward, he leaned in her window and smiled. "I'm handier than I look." His blue eyes flashed.

"I might have to keep you around," she said before her brain could weigh in.

Darn it.

If only words came tied to a string, so she could snatch the wrong ones back. "Anyway." She killed the engine. "Let's get the four wheelers unloaded."

Her mother and Neville crawled out of the rear, and the foursome congregated at the trailer. She unlocked the tailgate and her phone rang. She pulled it from her pocket and glanced at the screen. The manager at her Hattiesburg store. "Mama, wait on me. I need to get this." The unease gnawing at her all morning kicked into full-fledged anxiety. "What's up, Lucy?"

"There's been a little accident."

Her breath caught. "Define little."

"There was a fire at Donnie's Pizza next door. Our place suffered smoke and water damage."

Diana's heart sank. One of her smaller stores, not her biggest moneymaker. However, it employed several army wives from nearby Camp Shelby who relied on their part-time positions to supplement their spouses' income.

"All right, give me a few hours, and I'll be there."

Though leaving meant the end of her and Andrew's scheme. They'd never get another opportunity to demonstrate to Jackie and Neville the disaster they were sailing into. She couldn't let her mother enter a marriage doomed to fail.

"No, I've got it." Lucy's calm was one of the reasons she'd hired the sergeant's wife. "I wanted to let you know since I'm sure you'll need to make calls. I've rallied the ladies, and they're headed over to help sort through the mess. There's nothing you can do."

"Okay, if you're sure."

"We've got this. If we can handle two back-to-back deployments, a little fire is nothing."

After making the necessary call to her insurance agent, she rejoined the others. Her stomach rolled, but Lucy was right. Her ladies had it handled. "Well, hopefully we've had our glitch for this trip."

Andrew arched an eyebrow. "Everything okay?"

She eased the tail gate to the ground, creating a ramp to roll the four wheelers down. "Help me get these off, and I'll tell you about it."

Andrew followed Diana's lead as she explained the disaster that befell one of her shops. "I must say, you're taking this in your stride. Are you certain you can press on?" He wasn't keen for her to leave him to carry out their plan, but surely the cleanup was weighing on her mind.

"Thanks, but I'm good to go." She withdrew a roll of antacids then gestured to her mother and his uncle who were snogging at the side of the truck. "But for the love of all that's holy, can we please keep these two busy. I only have this one roll of antacids, and the nausea is killing me."

He could hardly blame her. Public displays of affection weren't his favorite either. "Uncle Neville, lend a hand, if you will."

The foursome strapped the remaining items to the all-terrain vehicles, and soon they were ready for departure. Andrew sidled up to

71

one of the vehicles, girding his loins for the task ahead. "Right then, which am I driving?" He'd never been on one before, but how difficult could they be to operate?

Diana's laugh cut him deeper than it should have.

"Hold on there, big boy." She patted the seat. "You and Neville get to be passengers. The terrain we're traveling is way too rough for a tenderfoot. This thing would buck you off within the first mile, and we're on our own once we leave the highway. Can't get cell service that far back in the woods."

His uncle's ruddy completion turned pallid. Even Diana cued into the fear crossing Neville's face. "Mama, you need to look after your fiancé. I'm not sure he likes the idea of roughing it. Perhaps this is asking too much of such a highfalutin man."

Jackie's brows knitted. "Is that right, Neville? I can't imagine anyone not loving the good Lord's creation. It seems heathen not to appreciate the wilderness."

Andrew leapt at the chance to drive a wedge between the couple, especially if it meant he didn't have to spend the next two days knee deep in the muck. On the other hand, it also required emasculating himself in the process. "It's not that we don't appreciate God's hand-iwork, Jackie. We're just not as hardy as the men are here in the South. From what I've seen, your men folk are a breed apart from those in other parts of the world. I'm sure this comes as a shock, but Uncle Neville and I don't measure up."

"Speak for yourself, boy." Neville jerked his fringed shirt in place. "I'll give it a go. Perhaps I'll find the rough and tumble life to my liking."

Jackie clapped her hands. "Oh, Dukie Dear, I do love you so."

Diana rolled her eyes as she passed around helmets. "Everyone mount up."

Following his uncle's example, Andrew climbed on behind his female counterpart. He'd settled on the seat when Diana fired up the machine and they bolted to a start. To counterbalance the sudden lurch forward, Andrew instinctively wrapped his arms around her waist. "Blimey." Falling off the back might have been preferable to his body's sudden reaction to so much contact with so many curves. He eased his hold and forced his thoughts elsewhere.

Three of a kind beats a pair. Flush beats a straight. Four of a kind, over a full house...

Ahead, the rutted path sent Jackie and his uncle bobbing about in a manner that would surely put Neville in need of aspirin at the end of the day—or a large gin and tonic. He seemed to be clutching his fiancé as tightly as Andrew had Diana.

Between anticipating the next jarring bump and dodging the occasional low-hanging limb, Andrew had quite enough to keep his mind off Diana's proximity. Suddenly, the pair in front hit a dip in the path, plummeting them so a good foot of light showed between the vehicle's seat and Neville's bottom.

Andrew let out a breath as the duo rocketed up the other side. He wished Diana had taken the lead, since their rear position afforded him the opportunity to brace himself and thus mitigate the blows to his posterior. Offering that suggestion wasn't possible given the noise of the engine and their helmets. Guilt tore at him despite the necessity of his uncle's trials.

As their surrounding shifted from a narrow path to wetlands, Andrew's field of worries narrowed to only the most basic. The dreaded stream lay ahead. Diana drove the all-terrain vehicle into the mud, and he latched on to her, praying to stay astride. Thick mud pelted his helmet and splattered his clothes the whole width of the bog. But truly, beyond the sensation of being nailed by small shot, his imagination made it out to be far worse than actuality. How often in recent memory had he the privilege of holding onto a lovely woman? If it weren't for their helmets occasionally knocking together, he'd have declared the journey well worth the effort.

On the far side of the bog from hell, Diana pulled alongside her mother. She raised the visor. "How's everyone doing?"

Jackie gave two thumbs up without looking behind her. "Good to go."

Perhaps she should have checked with her passenger. Uncle Neville's hands shook as he tugged his helmet off. "A spot of water wouldn't be amiss. Or something stronger if that's available."

Diana dismounted and moved to the rear of their vehicle. "I brought a little water for the road." She pulled a canteen from plastic tub strapped to the back and handed it to Neville. "A bottle of whiskey is buried deep in one of the other boxes, so that will have to be your incentive to make it to camp."

"It will occupy my every thought." After several sips, Neville handed the canteen back to Diana and replaced his helmet.

Jackie fired up the machine and took off as if a rack of brightly colored dresses waited for her ahead. Thus far, Jackie had doted on her fiancé. While annoying at times, it allayed Andrew's fears of her intentions. Climbing onto the all-terrain vehicle brought out a more mercenary side to the woman he liked even less than the scatterbrained version he first met at the airport.

"You good to go?" Diana's query penetrated his thoughts.

"I suppose. In for a penny. In for a pound."

"They'll be fine."

"Is your mother always so single minded?"

"I'm afraid so." She touched his arm. "Remember, this is the plan. They need to learn these things about each other. To see what *we've* known all along."

"I know, but I hate seeing him so miserable. He looked positively frightened."

Diana bit her lip. "That face of his broke my heart a little, but the way forward is better."

"At least the trail is."

"True. Let's mount up. Your uncle's going to want hot water to clean up and that's going to take a while."

Diana hadn't misled him. The path turned into an open meadow and beyond that, piney woods. Therefore, holding onto her wasn't a necessity. He did anyway. He gripped her slender waist. A certain rightness settled on him. The scenery wasn't bad either.

Well before Andrew was ready to let Diana go, they arrived at the much-lauded hunters' cabin. He'd pictured an Abraham Lincolnesque structure that would threaten to topple down upon them. Instead, he found a well-maintained house made of weathered boards and topped with a metal roof. A simple porch lined the front of two symmetrical boxes connected by a breezeway.

"What do you think of it? The part in the middle is called a dog trot," Diana explained. "The pen on the left houses a rudimentary kitchen and a lofted bedroom." She pointed to the opposite side. "This side has the other bedroom and a storage closet."

"It's quite nice. Humble but tidy. I can see guests wanting to come here for a getaway holiday." If it had electricity, running water, and plumbing, he might have found the place charming.

"Thanks. That's exactly what I was hoping for."

The joy in her voice caused him to turn in her direction. That smile of hers. His pulse hummed in his veins. A streak of mud decorated her cheek. Instead of marring her beauty, it accentuated her innate glow. Andrew took a step closer. His fingers itched to caress her cheek. If he did, what else would he want? He pointed to the smudge. "A bit of that mud seems to have found its way onto you."

"Mama always said I attracted dirt like a flower does a bee." Diana scrubbed it off and headed up the stone steps to the porch. "I better get a fire started so we can get cleaned up." She called over her shoulder. "Mama, you and Neville unload the four-wheelers. Andrew, you're with me."

Before complying with her command, he spared a moment to watch his uncle ease off the back of his seat like a man twice his years. Crossing the dog trot's warped floorboards, he entered the left side of the house. His eyes quickly adjusted to the low light, giving him a chance to assess the interior. A long, low cabinet ran the length of one wall, with a porcelain sink overlooking a window. A table and chairs took up the opposite wall. Ahead, Diana knelt before the open door of a black stove.

"Mind if I watch?" He took a knee beside her, fixated with the way she stacked small sticks into a tent shape.

"Be my guest." Using a single match and a twisted piece of newspaper, she set the kindling and pine straw alight.

The acrid scent first filled his nostrils, followed by sharp pine. "How did you manage to do that?" Tendrils of smoke danced up the stovepipe.

She chuckled. "You planning to take up backcountry living?"

"Hardly." He pointed to the steady flame ready for larger pieces. "It's nigh unto magic."

Diana handed him a piece of kindling. "This is fatwood. It's pine that's absorbed lots of resin, so it starts easily." She added a couple logs then closed the stove's door. "Let's fetch some water, now we've got that going."

"I don't about this *we* business. You're doing all the work."

With a backward glance at the stove, he followed her outside. He'd have tagged along behind her back through the mud pit if it allowed him to keep close. Could have watched her breathe simply for the pleasure of seeing her move. The economy of her motions, the quiet confidence, the joy she took in honest work.

She thrust a bucket at him. "Follow me down to the lake, and I'm warning you, you're going to get wet."

Andrew spread his arms to indicate the state of his clothing. "Like that matters at this point." He called to Neville who was carrying one of the plastic bins from the vehicle to the porch. "Be back shortly, Uncle."

The man lifted a weary hand. "Don't worry about me." He continued unloading the all-terrain vehicles.

But he did. "Will he be alright here?"

Diana looked around. "Most all the animals rest during the heat of the day, if that's where your mind was going." She called to Neville. "Did my mother say where she was off to?"

"No, my dear, she did not. Jackie gave me my marching orders and disappeared."

Andrew glanced around at the campsite. The bins needed unpacking, and they'd all want tea shortly. Where could the woman have gotten off to? He started to give voice to his question when he recalled Diana's description of the facilities. "I'm sure she'll turn up soon."

Diana nudged him. "Gathering water and purifying it is going to be a time-consuming process, so we need to get at it."

They followed a narrow path wounding its way through a grove of pine trees. As the lake came in view, so did Jackie. Quarter ways around the five-acre oval, the woman sat on the bank, fishing pole in hand. "She's off playing while she left my uncle to do all the work?"

"No." Diana cocked an eyebrow. "With any luck, she'll catch our dinner."

"And if she doesn't?"

She scooped up a bucket, passing it to him. "Worry not. Starving isn't part of the plan. I packed hamburgers in the cooler."

They made the return trip, with Diana pouring the water into a large cast iron pot on the stove. "At one time, this place had a good well, and my goal is to get it a new pump out here, so my guests can have running water. For the moment, we'll be kicking it old school." She pointed to a large plastic barrel by the sink and a canister-tube-spigot contraption. "Well, almost. I'm going to purify the water using these. Otherwise we'd have to boil all our water."

He peered inside the barrel and calculated how much it would take to get the mud off him and three other people. "I'll be on water duty."

She patted his arm. "Look at you being good for more than eye candy."

Andrew pondered Diana's remarks on the way down to the lake and back, wondering whether to consider them a compliment or insult. Either way, he'd managed not to say something stupid in return and only splashed half of one bucket down his front, so things were looking up. Eventually, he got steadier, and thanks to Diana's efficiency the campsite turned into a cozy little home.

On his final trip, Andrew found Neville seated in one of the front porch's rocking chairs. He changed out of his dirty clothes and cleaned up. "Uncle, you're looking much improved."

"Diana fixed me up." He lifted his feet from a pan of water.

The woman in question stepped onto the porch, passing Neville a beaker. "I made your tea the way I like my men." She winked. "Strong and sweet."

Neville took a sip and sighed. "I don't know when I've tasted anything better. Well done and thanks."

Andrew followed her back inside. "I thought our goal was to make him miserable."

She cringed. "I know, but the poor thing looked like death warmed over. And so lonely. He kept asking where Jackie was. I couldn't stand there and watch him suffer."

Tears pricked his eyes as the urge to take Diana in his arms nearly swallowed him whole. He wanted to chunk the whole scheme into the bin along with his return ticket home. Except—those weren't the plans. And his uncle's fiancée was proving quite callous toward him. Not that Andrew believed women should cater to men, but she could have at least shown him where to find a seat before she took off. "You're too kind."

She cocked her head. "Does that surprise you?"

"Not in the least." He took her hand. "But, remember our

mission."

"Don't worry. I forgot to pack the aspirin, so he'll be plenty hurting come bedtime."

"Speaking of which." He pointed to the loft. "Would you like me to sort things up there and across the way? I'm good with beds."

Diana blushed.

"I meant I always liked to help Nanny make my little bed, so I can actually cope without adult supervision."

"Sure, that would be great." She smiled. "By evening we'll be as cozy as four ticks on a hound dog."

Andrew cringed at the visual image. However, later that evening as he raised the last spoonful of Diana's skillet peach pie to his mouth, he couldn't help feeling a little like the aforementioned arachnid.

He and Diana had brought the table and chairs onto the dog trot allowing them to enjoy a bit of a breeze with their supper. She'd also set out several kerosene lanterns and candles, which added to ambiance. Earlier, he'd considered warning her against setting such a romantic mood, but both Neville and Jackie were in such foul tempers, it seemed strolling violins wouldn't get the two love birds back on the same page.

When he'd licked the spoon clean, he returned it to the bowl with a contented sigh. "If it weren't for every muscle in my body killing me, I'd say I was in heaven. Diana, I'll be dreaming of your pie for years to come."

And the woman who made it.

He savored their pudding just as he had the main course, a dish she called a "hobo tinfoil dinner." Jackie hadn't succeeded in her attempt to catch their dinner, and the failure put her in a petulant mood. She'd picked at the hamburger and potatoes, and now at her peaches. That was until movement underneath the table startled her. She squealed, giggled, and then leaned over to peck Neville's cheek.

Diana's bolted from her seat. "I've saved the best for last." She returned from inside with a bottle and four glasses. "We've earned a little indulgence tonight."

When she'd poured the whiskey and handed him his glass, Andrew saluted Diana. "To hard work and those who do it."

"To true love," his uncle countered. "And those who cherish it." He downed his drink and kissed his fiancée.

Those two were proving more resilient than he expected. "Fancy a stroll, Diana?" The need for a planning strategy outweighed his concern over nocturnal beasts.

She cut an eye at the couple. "Yeah." Grabbing a small torch, she led them outside. Once they were far enough away from the cabin, she let out a sigh. "I thought we had them for a moment."

"There's always tomorrow. We'll contrive an exercise to exhibit their unsuitability." Exactly what escaped him, especially as tiny flashing lights caught his attention. "What are those?"

"Fireflies, or here in Mississippi we call them lightning bugs. Want to catch them?"

"Not really." That was until she danced off into a thicket. He hadn't known Diana long, but this seemed uncharacteristic from the businesslike woman he'd been working with.

She returned, her hands cupped. "I used to do this with my friends all the time when I was little." Opening her fingers one at a time, she presented him with five glowing insects. "See. Aren't they darling?"

One flew off and landed in her hair. Its mates encircled Diana with a sparkling halo. "Positively enchanting." His breathe caught. The urge to kiss her came on strong. A quick taste of her lips, that's all. He leaned in. Only at the last moment did he gather the strength to resist. Protecting the family secret trumped personal desire. "We should get back to Neville and Jackie. God only knows what they're up to."

Diana ducked her chin. "Of course. Besides the skeeters are starting to eat me alive."

Andrew's heart pounded at the near miss. Somehow, he had to find a way of completing their mission—and keeping his head when it came to Diana.

Unease danced along Diana's skin. Unease having nothing to do with twilight turning to night. Unease not caused by the stirring of a possum in the tree above or the far away yip of a coyote. All those things were natural, predictable, recognizable. Unlike Andrew, who was muttering something about poker hands when he wasn't staring back at her, or tripping over the darkening path in a headlong rush back to the cabin.

His peculiar behavior followed them back to the porch where he dropped to his seat across from his uncle and poured himself a large quantity of whiskey. He downed half the glass in a long draw, before plunking it on the table and raking his hands through his hair.

Taking her seat across from him, Diana scrapped and stacked everyone's dishes. "I've already got some hot water going, so it won't take me long to get these washed up." What did it matter to her the reason for Andrew "coming over strange" as her grandmother would have called it? She had enough on her hands with her mother and Neville, who were whispering quietly to each other as if Diana and Andrew were invisible. "But I don't mind admitting right about now a dishwasher would be a divine thing."

Andrew lowered his glass. A drop of whiskey glistened on his lower lip. "Above indoor plumbing?"

His dark chuckle gave her goose bumps. "Maybe?" Diana tried not to return his smile. What was so amusing about ranking amenities? "Ask me again at midnight when I'm stumbling out back."

Their gazes connected, something passing between them. There it was again. The sloe-eyed look he gave whenever she made a joke. She leaned in. "You okay?" Was he sick?

"Certainly." He took a sip from the glass. "Why wouldn't I be?"

"You looked…" How? Like dinner didn't agree with him. Homesick? "Pensive."

"It's been a long day. That's all." His words came out in a lazy string just this side of a drawl.

"Speaking of long days." Jackie yawned and stretched. "I'm headed off to bed." She gestured toward the right pen housing the double bed.

"I'll be along shortly. Please don't hog the whole bed."

"Diana." Mama cocked her head.

"What? I don't want a repeat of when we went to Biloxi for your birthday. I'm too old to fall off the bed."

"Sweetie, you aren't the one who'll be my bedmate tonight."

"Oh." Her cheeks heated. It never occurred to Diana her mother and Neville would... She shook her head to clear away the mental image. "Mama, no." Embarrassment aside, if Jackie and Neville were intimate, it would be much harder to break them up. "What would Pastor Beecham think if he found out?"

Mama pursed her lips. "Who's going to tell him?"

Diana grasped for another rational. "What about Granddaddy Dansfield? You know he can see you from heaven." A wild excuse, true, but she was as low on options as a bride tardy to a Kleinfeld sale.

"Pish-posh."

"Don't you want to wait until your wedding night?" she asked, praying that particular horse hadn't already left the barn.

Finally, Andrew joined the fray. "As the future Duchess of Eff-ingham, you have to understand there's a proper way of doing things. One must keep up appearances."

Neville stood, holding Jackie's seat for her. "Well, my boy, Jackie and I are going to give the appearance of being a modern cou-ple."

"But Mama." Panic seized her chest. "That, that leaves me to bunk up with—"

Andrew choked. "Excuse me. Sorry. Went down the wrong way."

She cut her eyes at him. "I'm not any happier about it than you are; believe me." Why hadn't she thought this part through when she conjured up this brilliant plan? She massaged the twitch over her right brow. "Perhaps I can sleep out here on the porch."

Andrew waved away her offer. "No, I'll do it."

"Don't be ridiculous," Neville said. "We'll all be family soon, so there's nothing wrong with you two taking the loft."

Diana's stomach lurched. "Oh, my goodness—"

"—will not be relations." Andrew tossed back the rest of his drink.

"You two work things out however you like." Jackie took Neville by the hand. "We're retiring for the night." She pecked Diana on the cheek. "Sleep tight and don't let the bed bugs bite." With that she and Neville crossed to the other pen and closed the door.

"I'll be fine to sleep out here." Andrew smacked at a mosquito that landed on his arm, garnering a bloody smear for his efforts. "Really."

"No, what you'll be, is in need of a transfusion." She let out a breath. "Seriously, we're making a mountain out of a molehill. There are two twin beds up there." She took a stack of dishes inside and filled the sink with hot water.

Andrew followed with the remaining dishes, and after placing them with the others, took up position next to her at the sink. "True, and there's enough room to move them further apart if you feel uncomfortable."

"Not necessary." She handed him the first of the soapy glasses to rinse. "I doubt you're planning on ravaging me in my sleep."

He fumbled the glass, only barely saving it from crashing to the floor. "What? No! Why would you suggest a thing like that?"

"Ignore me. I'm making inappropriate jokes to cover for the fact my mother is across the way having sex. I never dawned on me she had that side to her life."

"I can understand. You've always been her caretaker, so your roles have been almost reversed."

"Nailed it exactly. Sounds like you have experience in that department."

"Not until recently." Their hands touched as she passed him another glass. "But I can see it's been a way of life for you."

There was that unease again, giving her goose bumps and making the hairs on her neck stand up. Maybe she was unaccustomed to empathy since folks in her world dolled it out with the same clenched fist as her grandmother did her famous Christmas divinity candy. The revelation still wouldn't make it any easier to pass the night a few feet from him.

After draining the sink, she dried off her hands. "All done here. I'll go up first and get into my PJs."

He swallowed hard. "Call when you want me to come up."

Upstairs, she took a moment to appreciate the tidy loft with its rustic furniture and white cotton curtains. Andrew had made up the side-by-side beds with matching summer-weight quilts. He'd even tucked the ends in with proper right-angle corners. Topping off his homemaking skills, he'd raised the windows at either end to draw a cross breeze and brought up a pitcher of water and two glasses.

Using the water from an old-fashioned pitcher and bowl, Diana cleaned up before slipping out of her jeans and T-shirt. Despite the cool water Andrew provided, a rivet of perspiration trickled down her neck as she reached around her back to unhook her bra. Even if the underwire hadn't been cutting into her all day, releasing the girls was one of the highlights of her evening. The edge of her favorite pair of shorty pajamas stuck out from the top of her duffle bag. Mocking her and the cool relief it could offer. Mocking her naïve belief Jackie led a chaste life. Mocking her for the attraction to Andrew that Diana could barely keep under control.

She riffled through the bag and pulled out a tank top and cotton shorts. "Thanks, Mother," she grumbled, slipping under the sheet. After lowering the lantern, she called to Andrew. "Come on up."

The wooden ladder creaked then his head peeked above the floor. "You decent?"

"Not according to the women at Greenville First Presbyterian, but I am fully clothed under this sheet."

He padded to his bed, sitting with his back to her. "I sense a story there." His shoes hit the floor. "I'd like to hear it if you will." He paused. Leaning across the bed he extinguished his lantern.

"Only if you share in return."

The soft rustle of clothes followed. "We will be up all night if you want to hear the tales of my misspent youth."

That was the idea. She needed something to get her mind off the damage to her store, a dozen itchy bug bites, and the fact her mother was shacked up across the way. "Tell me about your parents. Do you see them often?"

"I see them a few times a year when I come through London."

"Siblings?"

"I'm an only child as well. Eventually I'll inherit my father's title as well as Uncle Neville's."

"The weight of two dynasties rest fully on your shoulders."

"Too right. Some days it seems hardly worth the handful of titles it comes with."

And the money. Surely it took millions of pounds to keep up the estates and finance Andrew's playboy lifestyle.

"What about your *paterfamilias*?"

"My so-called father walked out on Mama and me. That's when we moved in with Granddaddy and Grandmother Dansfield. I haven't seen hide nor hair of my daddy since."

"Tell me about your grandparents. They seem to have been a positive influence on your upbringing."

"I can't imagine what my childhood would have been like without them. At the very least, they were my example of what a good and healthy relationship looks like. When I'm finally ready to settle down, I won't settle for anything less than what those two had—two equals working toward the same purpose."

The bed creaked as Andrew shifted. "I know the qualities I'm looking for in the next Duchess of Effingham, despite never having seen it in real life."

"I take it you're not referring to my mother."

"Are you doubting our plan?"

"No, just checking. Tell me about the lofty ideals this woman must attain to be found worthy. I assume you've got to choose someone with the same social standing."

"That's partly it. There are other criteria—more mercenary boxes to tick off. However, I have other expectations, a wish list of sorts, I believe will make us a good match."

"Let's hear them."

"I want someone who's kind, gracious, appreciates the past and those who carved it. She needs to love children and be committed to not only bringing forth the next generation but raising our children to be good people."

Surprise zinged through her. "She sounds—" Unexpected tears clogged her throat. "She sounds lovely." And the same qualities she wanted in a husband. "I hope you find her." She'd all but given up hope fate would send her such a man.

"Now it's my turn. I'd like to hear more about your grandfather. He sounds like quite the character, despite your assurances he would not have liked my uncle and me."

"I don't know…maybe he would have learned to tolerate you." She rubbed at the center of her chest. Three years later, it still hurt to talk about the most important man in her life. "I owe everything I am to my Granddaddy. He believed in me, gave me words of wisdom, and treated me like I was important." For a child growing up with a self-absorbed parent, this positive influence couldn't be underestimated.

"I feel the same way about my uncle. That man is more father—" Andrew cleared his throat. "Anyway, that's why I've been so protective about him."

"Speaking of which, how do you think he's doing?"

"He's uncomfortable; that's for certain, but he's not exactly miserable enough to throw in the towel."

"That's what I was afraid of."

"Jackie is completely oblivious to his limited experience, fatigue, or his sore muscles."

"Welcome to my world." At age six, she'd come down with chicken pox over a long weekend. It wasn't until she showed up at school covered in itchy scabs she'd received anything to relieve the discomfort.

"What are you going to do?"

"Me? How long is your uncle going to put up with that? She's my mother, so I'm stuck with her. He's still got options."

"You're right. Perhaps I'll have a word with him in the morning about standing up for himself. Like you said earlier, he should start out as he means to go on."

"Sounds like a plan." A warm breeze caressed her cheek. Her eyelids grew heavy.

In the distance, thunder rumbled. "Do we need to worry about that?" The scent of rain wafted in through the open window.

"Not unless it starts coming in through the windows."

Several moments passed with only the growing sound of thunder filling the air.

"Diana?" The low timbre of his voice reached across the room.

"Yes?"

"Do you still wish for a dishwasher over indoor plumbing?"

9

The next morning, Diana rose at first light to get breakfast going. With temperatures predicted in the high eighties, good sense required an early start in front of the stove. She'd closed the door on a pan of biscuits when Andrew descended into the kitchen. "Good morning." She finger-combed her rat's nest, wishing she'd taken a moment to run a brush through her hair. "I hope you slept well."

"Quite, thank you."

On him, the unkempt hair worked, and the whiskers made her want to run her hand along his jaw.

He grabbed a mug from the dish drainer then moved in close. "Your cheeks are bright pink."

"It's the stove." And maybe a little blushing. No one had a right to look that yummy first thing in the morning. "Breakfast will be ready soon."

He poured himself a cup of coffee then leaned against the cabinets. "The smell of bacon and coffee makes the absolute best alarm clock."

His snoring had woken her. Rather than annoying, she found the snuffling sounds of another human nearby comforting. She'd lain in the dark trying to remember the last time she'd been that close to a sleeping man. Counting back the months, she recalled a night eight months ago when she and Doc James took turns watching over a colicky horse. Which was sad, considering until six months ago, she was still dating Travis.

"I hope I didn't snore." His grin showed over the rim of the coffee cup. "I've been told I do."

She waved away his concern. "I only ask if you slept okay because when I woke this morning the windows were closed." And a light quilt had been thrown over her.

"It started raining in during the night." He took a long draw from the mug. "The sound of rain on metal is something else. I don't think I've ever heard a better lullaby."

Diana thought the same and hated she missed the rain song. "I must have been out. I didn't hear a thing. Then again, I always sleep well out here."

Andrew stretched. "The Ritz can't compare."

She laughed. "Now, now, it's starting to run up over the tops of my shoes. That bed wasn't that fabulous." Between turning the bacon and cracking eggs, Diana studied the viscount. He sure was agreeable for a man who'd endured a great deal of torture yesterday. She'd expected him to be at least as miserable as his uncle. Instead, he seemed to be relishing his exposure to rugged life. What was up with that?

"You see things your way, and I'll see them mine. I don't feel like I was dragged through the mud yesterday."

"Excellent, because I need you on your A-game today."

"What's the plan?"

She scooped up the scrambled eggs, placing them on a waiting plate. "I'm deciding between clearing a trail around the lake, so I can eventually bring the horses out here and doing cabin repairs."

"Which has the higher misery factor?" Andrew followed her lead, collecting the bacon and the dish of butter for the biscuits.

"Both have potential." Diana pointed through the door to the waiting table. "I vote we eat without the love birds. We can plan until they get out here."

After filling their plates and digging in, Diana began detailing her ideas. "Both require the same amount of physical strength and endurance. Sweating is a given. But if we stay around here, there are plenty of chances for everyone to take rest breaks. I'm leaning toward clearing the trail."

Andrew bit into a piece of bacon, his brow furrowing as he chewed. Finally, after a swig of coffee, he said, "I see your point, however, breaking a trail sounds more dangerous. Uncle Neville could get hurt or lost out there."

Before Diana could remind him of the impossibility of negating all danger, Jackie opened the door to the other pen and sashayed into the dog trot. She leaned down to peck her daughter's cheek. "Good morning, sunshine."

Diana rubbed her temple in the hopes of staving off the head-ache forming behind her right eye. "Mama, why are you wearing a dress?"

"I'm taking my sweetheart on a picnic. Dukie Dear endured quite a lot yesterday, and I don't want him to think this way of living is all rough and tumble."

"There are chores that need to be done around here, things I counted on y'alls help with. Boards have come loose around the back of the house. There are weeds growing up in the path to the outhouse. Not to mention the fact we need to get a couple machetes to the trail around the lake."

Jackie fluttered past on her way into the kitchen as if Diana's words were nothing more than butterflies tickling her ears. "I'm sorry, darling, you're going to have to adjust to not being my first priority anymore."

Anymore?! Irritation burned in Diana's stomach. Jackie's top priority had always been Jackie. She shot a pleading look to Andrew.

"Jackie, my uncle believes in duty over personal pursuits. I'm certain as much as he would enjoy spending time with you, he'd much rather not leave Diana in the lurch."

"Nonsense, my boy." Neville exited the bedroom, dressed in lightweight khakis, a plum colored golf shirt, and loafers on his feet.

"All work and no play."

Where the man kept acquiring his wardrobe baffled Diana. "How about a compromise? A few hours of work, and then we'll all take a picnic lunch down to the lake."

Jackie returned to the dog trot with a small hamper which she passed to the duke. She looped her arm through his and the two headed down the path to the lake. "We're going to the quail pasture to pick blackberries. Afterward, we'll have our picnic. I don't know when we'll be back, so don't wait on us to start your work."

The couple trod out of sight while Diana and Andrew sat speechless. How had the romantic duo outflanked them again? She wanted to pitch a good hissy fit and demand they come back, but her more sanguine partner in crime shook his head.

"It seems I'm not the only one who enjoyed the restorative powers of this cabin. I don't know how much you planned on charging for people to stay out here, but you need to consider upping the fees. I would have bet money the old chap couldn't have gotten out of bed today."

"Darn it all to heck." She growled. "I should have burned dinner last night."

"Too late for that. What do we do now?"

"Search me. Any chance your uncle is allergic to blackberries?"

"Loves the damn things." Andrew returned to his breakfast, proving the affinity ran in the family as he polished off the last of the homemade jam Diana carried at Sweet Tea and Lavender.

After cleaning his plate, he returned the dishes to the kitchen. Then he proceeded to wash up—like he'd been born pouring heated water from a kettle instead of with a bevy of servants waiting on him.

Alone all day in a cozy cabin with good husband material... Diana scrambled for a way to put distance between them. "Since Plan A is blown all the smithereens, I'm going to focus on situations I can control. At some point yesterday, the manager of the store in Hattiesburg texted me. I need to check in with her."

Andrew slung the dish rag over his shoulder and turned to face her. "I thought you said we didn't have cell service."

"It's spotty." She turned the phone around to show him the screen. "Certainly not enough to rely on in an emergency. I can't get my reply to go through."

"How is that something you can be proactive about?"

"Most of this area's pretty flat, but there's a high point about a quarter mile from here. I'm hoping that will be enough for me to get a good signal."

Andrew wiped out the cast iron skillet and put it back on the cook stove. "Would you like me to go with you?"

Images of playing house with him were hard enough to resist. Alone with Andrew in the woods...? Adam and Eve fantasies began playing in her imagination. "No offense, but there isn't much of a trail..."

"Say no more." He looked around the room. "Do you have something to drink, bug spray, compass?"

She held up a small backpack. "I've got everything I need right here."

He grabbed a box of power bars from off the counter. "Shouldn't you have a snack?"

"I won't be gone that long." Diana stepped out to the dog trot.

"Bear repellant?" he asked, following right behind.

She pointed to the pistol on her hip. "Right here. Although I'm hoping to avoid any encounters with Mrs. Yogi Bear or snakes for that matter."

He caught her hand as she was about to step off the porch. "How long do you think you'll be gone?" That pensive look she'd seen on Andrew's face last night returned. Only now, it made her want to smooth away his concern—with a kiss, or two, or a dozen. "I could be gone quite a while." At least until she had her hormones better under control.

At a bend in the trail, Diana chanced a look behind her. Yep. Andrew still stood in the middle of the path, reminding her of a beagle left from the hunt. Guilt needled her so bad she almost called for him to catch up. But that defeated half the reasons for her trekking up to the top of DeFrain's Hill in the first place.

Considering him simply a partner in preventing catastrophe was proving harder by the second, especially with certain *urges* muscling in on her good sense. As much as she'd have rather spent time making improvements around the hunters' cabin, hanging around a place with so much privacy sounded like regret waiting for a place to happen. "I need another playboy in my life like a pig needs a sidesaddle."

Low hanging limbs and patches of briars slowed her progress, as did the need for constant vigilance for snakes. She shuttered all over at the thought of the stealthy critters. Before every step, Diana scanned the undergrowth for copperheads and tuned her ears for the telltale rustle of a large mammal. Bears nudged snakes out of the top spot of critters to avoid.

Cresting the rise, Diana's phone sprang to life. "Jeez, Louise." She jumped out of her skin at a series of pings pierced the quiet. Feeling justified for making the hike up the hill, she slid her finger across the screen and read the messages, beginning with the ones from Lucy, the store manager in Hattiesburg.

Cleanup crew arrived

Damage to stock minimal

Serve-Pro company arrived

All done. I'm locking up

"So much for finding an excuse to stay up here. Darn your efficiency." Next, she checked the other messages, finding one from Jasmine.

Back among the living. So sorry for letting you down. I heard what your mother did. All my fault so I'll resign.

Her fingers couldn't bring up the event planner's number fast enough. When the call connected, she didn't give Jasmine the chance to say hello. "Like heck you're quitting on me."

Jasmine chuckled, still sounding weak from a bout with stomach flu. "Hello to you too. Are you back already?"

"No, we'll stay another night."

"How are the fancy men fairing?"

After giving a nearby log a thorough examination, Diana sat

down. "They're fine, dagnabbit. That stiff upper lip is a real thing. I've done everything I can think of short of poison or letting them get lost in the woods."

"Maybe you should consider the latter. Otherwise…"

An image of a tiara-wearing mama parading around the duke's estate popped to mind. That wasn't as bad as the duke's cowboy imitation. Diana took a drink from her water bottle and pondered the possibility of having to resort to low tactics. She hated the idea of stooping to underhanded dealings. Granddaddy Dansfield raised her better, but her ox was in the ditch. "Andrew says that's off limits. We can't put his uncle in physical danger."

"Ahhh, so sweet. Looks and a good heart. Unlike Travis." Jasmine derision carried across the connection.

"Don't remind me." Diana's former boyfriend's attraction could be compared to a large chocolate layer cake. Yummy. Decadent. Ultimately bad for you.

Jasmine had cued into the town's newest attorney, despite his trappings of success. When he'd been caught doing Diana's best friend in the backseat of her daddy's pickup truck, Jasmine offered to arrange an accident for him. Diana had laughed off the offer but made a mental note not to do anything to anger the woman.

"Oh, by the way," Jasmine continued. "Megan's knocked up. Showed up at Zumba class with her bump showing, just as proud as can be."

Suddenly, Diana regretted not giving Jasmine's offer more

consideration. "If she even thinks about asking us to do her a baby shower, I won't be responsible for my actions."

"I've got your back, boss. I'll toss her skinny-jeans-wearing behind out before she can get up the front steps."

Between Mama's shenanigans and coming down with a crush on Mr. Viscount, her life was one steaming pile of donkey dung. "Tell me something else. I need to get my mind off things."

"Where are you calling from? I thought there wasn't any cell service at the cabin."

Diana adjusted her position on the log, settling in for one of their good conversations. "There isn't. I climbed up DeFrain's Hill to check on a situation with one of the stores. That's all handled so now I can talk."

"Why aren't you back at the cabin talking to Andrew?"

"It's complicated."

"Oooh, complicated is my favorite. Spill it."

She let out a breath. "He's just so…" A loud rusting caught her attention. She paused. It grew closer. "Wait. I hear something." Off to her left a wild-growing rhododendron shook. "Crap, Doc James said there was a bear around. I have to go."

"Call right back." Her voice pitched higher. "This is why *normal* people don't play in the woods."

The huffing and snuffling got louder. Diana withdrew her pistol from its holster and flicked off the safety. The last thing she wanted was to kill a mama bear, but she also didn't want to end her days as bear poop.

Her heart pounded. Feet itched to run. But, even a tenderfoot knew doing so would only incite the bear's chase instinct. "Ya, bear. Go away. Scat." Holstering the gun, she picked up a nearby limb and rattled it.

The rustling grew nearer. She took cover behind a tree. "Bear be gone."

"Bear?" Andrew burst through the brush, looking behind him. "Where? I thought I got away from it."

"What?" She latched onto him. "You saw it? Where?" The closest she'd ever come to a bear was at the zoo. Realizing how near he'd come to getting mauled, she squeezed him hard.

"Down by some blackberry bushes. She had two little cubs."

He'd been wandering in the woods on his own, the one tactic he'd firmly placed off-limits for use on his uncle. "That's half a mile away. What were you doing over there?" Anger flared to life. "More to the point, what are you doing here? Did you think you needed to rescue me?" She shoved him away and wagged her finger in his face for good measure. "Let me tell you, I know my way around these woods as well as I do Greenville Mall."

Andrew folded his arms. "Are you finished?"

"Yes." The sudden burst of temper left her breathing hard.

"I, I finished the chores, and Uncle and Jackie still weren't back, and, well..." He toed the ground with his shoe. "I missed you." He looked up, catching her gaze. "Alright, I said it, I missed you. I'd been having so much fun at the cabin, and once you left you took all the fun with you."

Diana's insides melted like chocolate in cobbler, fresh from the oven. If Travis had ever said something like that, she'd have clawed Megan's eyes out before she'd let her former best friend steal him away. "Why is it you don't have a girlfriend?"

"I don't exactly meet the type of woman I'm expected to marry in my everyday life."

"You never have told me what you do to occupy your time." His past had so many holes in it, it resembled chicken wire. Did she want to risk getting involved with a professional loafer when she needed Mr. Plan Ahead?

"That's not important now." He stepped closer, taking her hands in his. "What is…important is…we need to make the most of our time here."

"How to you suggest we do that?" Her heart pounded, mouth went dry. Did a plan for the next half hour count?

"By this."

Andrew tilted her chin and lowered his mouth to hers. The press of lips started gently, as if he might stop at any moment. He didn't. Thank God. Instead, he threaded his fingers through her hair and deepened the kiss. In response, Diana twined her arms around his middle and brought him in close. The feel of firm muscles caught her by surprise, as did the scent of good, clean sweat and pine. He peppered kisses across her cheek and down her neck, and when he finally pulled away, he had to hold her steady.

A smile turned up the corner of his mouth. "I've been thinking about doing that since last time."

"Me, too." She rested her forehead against his chest. "That's why I came out here."

"There aren't any problems with the store?"

"There were. I didn't deceive you. I'm an honest person. Some say too honest, but I'm not above killing two birds with one stone."

Andrew tilted her chin. "I believe you." He brushed a stray curl from her face before kissing her again.

"Lord have mercy." She could let him do that all day and twice on Sunday. She pushed out of his embrace. "Wait a minute. Just because your kisses make my eyes roll up in the back of my head doesn't mean I'm following my mother's example."

His expression fell. "Oh, I thought perhaps."

"Who am I kidding?" She let out a breath. "I'd like for you to do that again, all right."

"You would? But what about—?"

"I'm going to quote a much-lauded southern literary character, 'I'll worry about that tomorrow.'"

His dimple flashed when he smiled. "I can do that. I so can do that, too."

Hand-in-hand, they started down the hill toward the cabin. "We can follow my marks if you like." He pointed to several trees standing yards apart.

"You marked a path?" Diana stepped to the closest, examining a white mark scratched into the bark of a large oak. "What did you use?"

"Chalk. It was either that or crumble your leftover biscuits, and those are too good to waste."

She followed the marks with her gaze as they zig-zagged across the woods. "Good strategy, but we'll be out here all day if we follow your path." She pointed to her trail of broken pine saplings. "If we go my way, it's all downhill."

Andrew chuckled. "I hope that's not a metaphor for your plans to stop the wedding."

She elbowed him. "I'll have you know—"

"Oww, I take it back." He drew her in closer, wrapping her arm around him. "We've got tonight to come up with another plan. I'm feeling desperate in the face of their resistance to our tactics. After your mum and my uncle retire for the evening, we can have an emergency planning meeting."

"Doesn't sound as much fun as last night's pajama party."

"Speaking of sleepovers." He wagged his eyebrows. "How do you feel about rearranging the furniture in the loft?"

"I'm not averse to redecorating."

Andrew increased the pace. "Excellent."

If only their plans for preventing a catastrophic marriage could be worked out so easily. Diana devised and discarded half a dozen wedding-stopping plans while remaining vigilant for snakes and bears. It would be her luck to come this close to a little happy time with Mr. Viscount only to have something like a snake bite or a bear encounter get in the way.

As they joined the trail leading to the lake, shouts caught her attention. "That's my mama." Staccato words punctured the air like a machine gun. "Lordy Jesus, she's mad as heck about something." Diana grabbed ahold of Andrew's hand and took off running in the direction of the commotion. When they reached the open field where the couple was supposed to have picnicked, another voice joined Jackie's.

"That's my uncle. He's in pain." Diana and Andrew raced in the direction of the caterwauling, finding the other couple hobbling around a bend in the trail, soaking wet, and arguing like two dogs with one bone.

"Darn fool man." Jackie held on to Neville by the waist, dragging him along. The bloom was well and truly off the romance as she continued her rapid-fire recriminations. "...the good sense God gave a goose."

Neville grumbled, favoring his right leg. "What did you expect me to do?"

"Mama, what happened to y'all?"

Jackie's wrath wasn't the duke's only issue. Angry welts dotted his face and arms, and droplets of blood trickled from several deep scratches.

"Smarty Pants here got himself tangled up in the blackberry

bushes." She foisted her fiancé onto Andrew, jerking her wet sundress back into place. "And his solution was to go off running into a yellow jacket nest." Jackie locked arms with Diana and turned her back on the men.

"And this delightful woman decided our best option for escape was to take a swim in the lake."

Jackie jerked around. "Got 'em off of you, didn't I?" Then she resumed her march back to the cabin.

"At the risk of sounding ungrateful, I'm not sure drowning was a preferable option. We could have outrun them."

"Who are you kidding? You couldn't outrun an overfed, three-legged coon."

"Which we ran into, by the way," Neville added.

Diana turned around to tell Andrew it was a good thing they hadn't encountered any of the traps that had likely relieved the raccoon of its leg. However, one look at the duke's face and her words dried up.

His lip quivered. "My boy, did you know this forest is full of strange creatures. It's like rejects from Noah's ark all congregated here." His voice pitched high with emotion.

"I don't know about that, Uncle." Andrew caught Diana's gaze. "I've found the woods here to be quite enchanting."

Despite the circumstances, all Diana could do was grin back like a goof. "I'm glad I could broaden your horizons." Thank heavens her mama was as self-absorbed as ever.

Jackie jabbed a finger in Andrew's direction. "See, even your fancy-pants nephew is smart enough to appreciate the good Lord's creation. Unlike some men I know. And I use the term loosely."

"No, Mama. There's no call to question the duke's masculinity. That's hitting below the belt."

Diana increased the pace, putting enough distance between Jackie and the duke to give the poor man relief on at least one front. Once the guys reached the cabin, she turned her attention to Neville's injuries. The cuts required only a good cleaning, but the yellow jackets had done a number on him. "Let me get you inside, and I'll put a compress on your stings."

Andrew nodded toward Jackie. "Perhaps a better idea would be for us to divide along family lines."

Jackie's protruding bottom lip quivered a warning of an impending tearful tirade. They were mere seconds away from a full-Jackie-Curtis meltdown. Diana's natural inclination was to cut the tantrum off at the pass.

She couldn't afford to waste this golden opportunity, could she?

She shot a questioning look to Andrew, hoping for insight on how to best to take advantage of the situation. Direct insults to Neville could send her contrary mother back into her lover's arms. No one enjoyed praise more than Jackie.

"You know, Mama, you did the right thing back there. That was quick thinking, even if it's gone unappreciated. Now, let's get you out of those wet clothes." Continuing to lay it on with a trowel, she escorted a whimpering Jackie over to the other pen. "It's right difficult when men don't give us women the credit we deserve. Why, that man would most likely be dead of anaphylaxis shock if it weren't for you. You saved his life."

"I did, didn't I?" Jackie shucked out of her wet dress and pulled on a pair of sweats.

"Why don't you lie down for a while?" Diana pulled down the light-weight quilt and patted the bed. "A nap will do you good."

Once she had the covers pulled up to her mama's chin, she stepped back. Andrew could manage first aid for his uncle but mixing up the witch hazel and baking soda was beyond his scope of experience.

Jackie caught her hand. "Stay." She patted the place next to her. "I haven't gotten to spend any time with you lately."

Diana managed to catch the "whose fault is that?" response before it left her lips. She cocked her hip against the bed. "Okay. For a little while. I want to get your lunch going soon."

"Did I do a good job with the wedding?"

"You certainly made it memorable." For all of Greenville. "And your problem solving was definitely outside the box."

Jackie's eyes drifted close. "I'm glad you're proud of me."

The last sentence cut deep. For most of her life, embarrassment and protectiveness and obligation defined their relationship. It never dawned on Diana her mama gave their relationship a passing thought, much less she wanted her daughter to feel pride in her mother.

Diana patted her mother's cheek. "You did good." With that, she tiptoed over to the other side where she found Andrew at the stove and Neville waiting at the table.

She handed the duke the dry clothes she'd scooped up on the way out. "I'll make you that compress now."

He lowered a cloth he had pressed to his face. "Thank you." With his left eye nearly swollen shut and his cheeks dotted with red welts, his aristocratic lift of the chin lost its frost.

Andrew presented his uncle with a steaming mug. "And here's your tea."

At the sink, she mixed the ingredients for the plaster in one of their coffee cups. After getting the baking soda and witch hazel the right consistency, she motioned for Andrew. "This and a couple anti-histamines from the first-aid kit should relieve the pain from his stings."

He poked the mixture and muttered, "Not much to be done for the tongue lashing he got."

"I know, but that was our plan."

"Then why do I feel like such an ass?" He nodded in the direction of the other pen. "How's she doing?"

"I finally got her down for a nap. Before that, she was tearful and wounded. My mama's not accustomed to folks not appreciating her efforts, as minimal as they may be."

"He's the same way. Everyone's so deferential with him."

She laced her fingers with his. "I know it weighs heavy on you, but you and I are doing the right thing."

He turned to face her, a small smile teasing his lips. "To which thing are you referring? Because as of now, I believe our plans for this evening have been cancelled."

"I think we should head back to Greenbrier anyway. The further apart we keep these two, the better. Goodness knows, we don't want all our hard work coming undone." She crossed the room to the duke. "After you get out of your wet clothes, let Andrew smear the compound on your stings." She pointed to the door. "I'll step outside to give you privacy."

Andrew nodded. "I'll come help you load the vehicles once I'm finished here."

Out in the dog trot, the energy that had gotten her through the day's drama bombs drained out of her like a blow-up swimming pool with a big ole hole in the side. She plopped down on the front steps and buried her face in her hands. All her life's choices were made to achieve stability and security. In the space of four days, Jackie had blown her carefully constructed life to kingdom come. To say nothing of what Mr. Viscount was doing to whatever remained of her good sense—and heart. "Why couldn't you be a jerk face like Travis?"

"You talking to me." Andrew joined her on the step, sitting a little nearer than was good for her wits.

"More like pondering the universe."

"What are your plans for returning to Greenbrier?"

"You feel confident enough to drive one of the four-wheelers?"

He cringed. "I'll do a passable job, but I have to admit a bit of arrogance fueled my prior confidence."

"A bit?" She chuckled. "Sugar, you have confidence oozing out your pores."

"Am I allowed to tell one of the reasons behind my wanting to drive?"

"It wasn't male pride driving your desire to be behind the wheel?"

"Only partially. Now that I've allow myself to fully appreciate my position, I won't get that second chance."

"It's for the best."

"Can I say how weary I am of hearing that phrase?"

"Me too." She patted his knee. "Let's get packed up. As soon as Mama wakes, I want us ready to go."

"Mud bog, here I come."

"The fun really starts once we get back."

Andrew cocked an eyebrow. "What can I expect when I get back to Greenbrier?"

What can I expect when I get back to Greenbrier?

Andrew's double entendre query still burned in Diana's ears hours after ferrying the group back to civilization. So far there'd been a scene where Mama threw her engagement ring at Neville, a fuming and humiliated duke being dragged off by his nephew, and a minor crisis over an upcoming baby shower to be held in the gardens. But nothing in the way of making good on their plans for another sleepover.

Long after nightfall, Diana was still trying to get Jackie down for the night. She feigned a yawn hoping it might work where the warm milk and hot bath hadn't. "I think I hear my bed calling my name."

Jackie stared at the TV where her favorite show, *Designing Women,* had played continually for the past several hours.

"Aren't you tired? It's been a long day." Diana tapped into her mother's sense of martyrdom. "And you've endured a lot today. A good night's sleep is exactly what you deserve."

"Bed. Coffin." Jackie sniffled. "What difference does it make? That man has slain me with his ingratitude. I don't know how I'll face him in the morning. My heart is broken. It didn't hurt this much when your daddy ran off."

Diana barely managed to stop the eye roll as she stepped to the bathroom to retrieve her mother's nightly medication. Most of what Jackie took was vitamins and herbal supplements, the exception being a prescription sleep aid. Diana added a couple aspirin for the muscle aches her mother was complaining about. If luck was on her side in any kind of way, her mama would sleep until noon tomorrow. "Here are your pills. You get some sleep and don't worry about a thing. I'll take care of our guests."

After Jackie closed her bedroom door, it seemed to take forever for the light to disappear from beneath it. "Finally." Now she knew how a new mom felt. Diana typed out a text to Andrew. Then deleted it. If she had any sense, she'd go to bed. Alone. Instead, she ran a comb through her hair, dabbed on lipstick, and went in search of her viscount.

Up in the original part of the mansion, she knocked on the door of the Azalea Suite. No answer. "God, you're telling me something, aren't you?" The words of her Sunday School teacher, Mrs. Whitener, came to mind. "Only a fool chases after trouble."

Diana rapped at the door again. To be sure. Andrew wasn't trouble. Not in the way Travis was. Andrew had many fine qualities her ex would never possess even if he lived to be a hundred. There simply wasn't a future with Andrew. "But what if I don't want forever? There's no harm in two people…" She couldn't say it out loud, so she shouldn't be doing it. "I'm a modern woman, and there's no harm in Andrew and me enjoying each other's company for the evening." When Andrew didn't answer, she looked for him in the lounge and by the pool. No hunky viscount in either location.

Diana cast her eyes skyward. "I see you've weighed in on the subject. Fine, I'll go back to my room."

As she walked down the corridor toward the family quarters, a head of dark hair caught her attention.

Opportunity or temptation?

The fates certainly put him in an unlikely spot. She hit reverse, sliding into the business center. Andrew sat in front of a computer screen. With a furrowed brow and the addition of glasses, her playboy took on a businesslike air. She closed the distance, catching the scent of the hotel's peppermint soap radiating off him. "Need anything?"

Andrew closed out the page, looked up, and flashed a smile—one that didn't quite reach his eyes. "I'm good. Just checking in back home."

"I shouldn't interrupt."

"You're not." He tugged her down to the chair next to him. "You're my favorite distraction."

"What do you need to be distracted from? Other than the obvious."

There was that chiseled smile again. "Not a thing. How's your mum?"

"Appropriately medicated. I made certain she took her sleeping pill. Jackie Curtis isn't going anywhere tonight. The duke?"

"Properly inebriated as to have him off our hands for the night." He rubbed his brow. "Do you get the sense we're the parents to mischievous toddlers?"

"Welcome to my world."

"Let's celebrate our liberty with a drink." He took her by the hand, sending a surge of electricity up her arm. "I think your bar is still open."

At the front of the mansion, they entered the former parlor. Diana had decorated the cozy space in dark red and gold in keeping with Victorian color schemes. Crossing the dark-stained oak floors, Diana grabbed a bottle and two glasses from behind the bar. She pointed to a small alcove, one of her favorite spots in the whole house. "We'll have plenty of privacy in here."

Andrew's hand never left the small of her back. He held her chair. "Privacy is exactly what I'm looking for." After she'd sat, he moved his chair so they both faced the bay window. Then, he wrapped his arm around her shoulder.

The nearness had her stomach doing backflips. She uncorked the scotch, pouring the amber liquid as slowly as if it were gold.

Would she go through with this knowing it would lead nowhere?

Andrew stretch out his legs. "I see now why you like this location so much." He took a sip from his glass then played with her hair. "The monkey wallpaper, the heavy oak furniture. It screams colonial Africa."

The prospect of making love certainly didn't have him in knots. "Have you ever been?"

"Tanzania during my gap year."

Gap year. She'd begun dual enrollment her junior year of high school. Working evenings and weekends, she'd also taken as many courses as her adviser would allow to graduate at twenty. "That must have been interesting."

His jaw ticked. "I had many informative experiences and learned many skills that year."

While her world encompassed a hundred-mile radius from her current location.

Andrew was so easy to talk to she forgot how far out of her league he was. The knowledge did nothing to quench her simmering desire. Was this how her mother had fallen for the duke? It certainly wasn't Diana's typical romantic course of action. Travis had never given her goose bumps. "During the day you can see the koi pond from here."

Sadness flashed in his eyes. "Another beauty I won't be able to indulge in. I wish I was going to be here to enjoy it with you."

Me too. "What time will you leave in the morning?"

123

"I have a car coming at half past five."

Diana swallowed her emotions. How provincial of her to become attached to someone after a handful of days. She held up her tumbler. "Here's to our success."

He touched her glass with his. "And to many more successes. I'm a great admirer of yours. I would do well to emulate your practices."

Curiosity lured her like a cat watching birds from the wrong side of a window. "How do you mean? I can't imagine how my life could apply to yours."

Andrew leaned in, kissing her lightly on the lips. "I'd rather not dwell on business, especially not when I have such a lovely lady in my presence."

A giggle escaped Diana's lips before she could catch it.

"What?" His expression darkened. "You doubt my sincerity? Quite insulting to my character as a gentleman."

She covered her mouth, again too late to trap an unladylike noise. "Sorry. Nerves." Goodness gracious, she'd come down with a case of the sillies. "I promise I won't be like this the whole time."

That was very presumptive of me.

Perhaps Andrew no longer wanted a fling—especially with someone acting as if they didn't have two brain cells to rub together. "I mean, I'm not usually like this. It must be the scotch."

He leaned closer. "You should behave in any fashion that strikes your fancy. God knows you've got reason enough to need a laugh."

His lids lowered to half-mast. "As do I."

Who knew blue eyes could smolder? Was it possible to melt and combust simultaneously? She fanned herself with the hand he wasn't holding. There certainly was enough heat going on in the tiny alcove.

"I propose we adjourn to my suite." His gaze cut to her glass. "If you're not feeling the effects of drink overmuch."

"No, no, I'm fine." Diana couldn't get the words out fast enough. "I've only had a couple sips." Although now her nerves were running the show, a shot sounded like a good idea. She rejected the impulse. Making love with Andrew would be a one-off, and she didn't want alcohol to dull the experience. "Lead the way."

He held her chair, then as before, his hand went to the small of her back as they crossed the parlor. The room was empty of guests, whose curious stares would matter less than her bartender's. She waved to Randall on the way out, figuring news of the boss's nocturnal escapades would reach every member of staff by morning. Although, once Mama rose and turned on the waterworks, the staff would be too busy catering to and/or avoiding Jackie.

In the foyer, Andrew stopped at the front desk. "Please arrange for a wake-up call to His Grace's suite."

They'd caught the middle-aged woman enjoying a diet cola and playing on her phone, causing her to choke on the former and fumble the later. "Excuse me." She blushed from her neck to her ears.

Some of Melanie's color also might have come from the charming way Andrew leaned against the antique desk.

"What time, sir?"

"Half past four should suffice."

"And you, sir?"

"That won't be necessary." He cut his gaze to Diana. "I don't imagine I'll need waking."

Now it was her turn to blush. She swatted Andrew's hand. The one creeping south to her bottom. "Thanks for giving Meddling Melanie something to do besides solitaire. She'll be on the phone to my chef before we're up the stairs."

He stopped midway up the stairs. "Why would you retain a gossip, especially one who does so about her employer?"

"She's a distant relative with more problems than a dog's got fleas."

"But why do you care so much about her opinion if she's got her own issues?"

They continued onto the second floor. "In a town as small and conservative as Greenville, it's not only a woman's reputation she has to worry about. If the right people feel I'm disreputable, I'll lose business."

They reached the Azalea Suite. "If you're not comfortable with this, I'll understand."

Should she take the next step? The one well outside her comfort zone. "I can risk it." But could she risk her heart?

He arched an eyebrow. Ever the gentleman.

Anticipation danced along her skin. "Open the dang door."

Diana scanned the hallway, expecting guests to tumble out of their rooms. She whispered. "I promise the Lady's Sewing Circle won't be quilting a letter A on my shirt."

When he smiled, a spark of mischief lit his eyes. "As long as you're sure." With that, he flung open the door and scooped her into his arms.

She squealed. "Put me down."

Andrew kicked the door closed, crossed to the bed, and tossed her in it. "As you wish, milady."

The giggles came back with a vengeance. "If we break my grandmother Dansfield's bed, she'll come back to haunt me."

He kicked off his shoes then prowled across the bed. Arching over her, he kissed her long and deep. "We certainly wouldn't want that." Moving the length of her body, he tugged off her sandals. And nibbled her toes. He trailed his hands up her bare legs to the edge of her shorts.

Thank God I shaved above the knees.

Between kisses, caresses, and more than a few giggles, she shimmied out of her clothes. Then she went to work on his. Going slowly like she was unwrapping the best Christmas present ever. Finally, she had him down to a pair of boxer briefs. She'd vaguely wondered what British aristocracy wore in the way of underwear, and now she knew.

Andrew slid the briefs down his hips—and all ponderings and giggles fled.

"Oh. My. Gawd." She slid under the covers, and he joined her.

The next several minutes flew by in a passionate rush. After catching their breath, the second act moved with more intention and tenderness. Finally, he held her to his chest, tracing circles across her back. She tried to stay awake, but her eyelids grew heavier than those darn kettlebells at the gym.

A quick nap and then perhaps there'd be time for a finale. After all, she could sleep after Andrew and his uncle had left. The last thing she recalled was the press of his lips to her hair.

Andrew lay next to Diana, wishing he could keep the sun from its progress. With each moment it brought color to the room, it also drew closer the hour of his departure. "Named after a princess and a goddess. That's one thing your mum got right."

Sympathy for his uncle's situation grew. The Curtis women had charm in spades. Only the lovely woman sleeping next to him also had brains and a tender heart to match. "A fine mess you've gotten yourself in, Montgomery."

Diana snuggled closer, throwing her arm across his middle. He could spare a few moments before he and Uncle Neville departed for the airport. "How do I hold on to you?"

As the room grew brighter, the portrait of Diana's ancestor became visible. During his first night at the mansion, Andrew had studied the man and the short biography below the frame. The riverboat captain and he had much in common. Risk taker. Rambler. Rake. Would having a gambler for an ancestor make her more receptive to Andrew's profession? Or less so?

She placed great import on stability and security. Two virtues she deserved, and he lacked. Except when it came to his feelings for her. Given half a chance, he'd prove how much she could count on him in that regard.

What could he offer her? A title? And a decaying estate that went with it. Over the years he'd won enough to replace the roof and install a heating system keeping his uncle from freezing. That still left overgrown woods, a century-old greenhouse needing razing, and plumbing straight out of the Dickens era.

Diana had given him plenty of inspiration for ways to make his uncle's estate profitable. "I wonder how well-paid tours of the house and gardens would do?" He could also consider opening the grand hall for functions. Following Diana's business plan would take time but at the end of the day, he'd have more to offer her than a title with no money behind it.

"What I need is seed money." Which meant returning to the casinos as soon as he got Neville settle back at Chatham Park.

Could he become the man she deserved before someone better suited wooed her away?

Andrew's low murmurings stirred Diana from her sleep. She kept still, playing possum, in the hopes he'd tell Great-Great-Great Grandpa Dansfield something important. Nothing but ramblings about the family estate unrelated to the one thing she most wanted to know. Would he want to make plans to see her again? If not, there might be a pity party for two later that morning.

Darn it all. Falling in love wasn't in my five-year plan.

"Father and Uncle can bugger off if they don't like it. If I can manage it, their opinion be damned."

Diana silently urged him to continue, but it seemed he'd made up his mind. And Great-Great-Great Grandpa Dansfield wasn't weighing in. She kissed the underside of his chin. "How long until the car comes?"

Wanting a moment in the bathroom, to at least brush her teeth, she attempted to ease from beneath the covers.

"We have less than an hour." He tugged her back. "I'd like to make the most of it, but first I have a question."

Her pulse raced. Did she dare hope? "Okay." If he wanted to take home a jar of Sweet Tea and Lavender's blackberry jam she wouldn't be responsible for her actions. "Ask away."

"Do you think I could see you again?" He kissed her temple, his tenderness conveying much more of his feelings than his simple request had. "I don't know how we'd pull it off—"

Relief spread through her whole body. "Where there's a will, there's a way." She hadn't been wrong in making the leap into bed with him. After a quick kiss, she pulled away, grabbed her clothes from the floor, and dressed. They needed to at least make rudimentary plans before he and his uncle left.

"Neither my uncle nor your mother will see this as anything other than a betrayal."

She slumped back to the bed. "I know." Guilt knotted her stomach like cold, thick oatmeal. "We'll have to be discreet."

"Last night notwithstanding, discretion is my middle name."

"Another tidbit of information about my mysterious lover." Would she ever know any more about him than she currently did?

"No great mystery, simply a string of meaningless details." He captured her face with his palms then kissed her slow and deep.

Jackie's heartbreak tempered Diana's joy. Her mother would need her more than ever. "Can we say our goodbyes here? I think under the circumstances it would be better if we kept things lowkey."

"I couldn't agree more." He kissed her again, making her hope they'd be able to contrive a rendezvous soon. Finally, she gathered the strength to pull away. "I'll leave you to get ready."

"What will you do?"

"Distract Mama. The last thing anyone needs is another scene. I, for one, have had enough melodrama to last a lifetime."

"I'll ring you tomorrow. We'll make plans. Something firm. A date. A place."

She nodded. They'd known each other a handful of days, so the amount of emotion bubbling inside her had to be from all the mama-drama. Squaring her shoulders, she slipped from the room and headed back to the family quarters.

Of course, on the other side of the door there had to be one of her chambermaids. "Good morning, Sally. The Azalea and Magnolia Suites will be vacant shortly, and you'll be able to get in there."

The young mom lifted an eyebrow. "Should I simply make the beds or put on fresh sheets."

To make Greenbrier green, the rooms received new sheets only when a guest departed. "Please give both rooms a thorough going over." A worry bloomed to life. "And if His Grace should leave any notes or tokens behind, please give them to me, not my mother."

"Got it." Sally's knowing nod gave Diana all the information she needed. Every person in the mansion knew Mama's wedding was off. By noon, the whole town would know Jackie had made a fool of herself. All along she'd wanted to avoid such an event occurring.

As she hurried through the hallways, Diana considered one diverting activity after another. She discarded shopping, horseback riding, or a visit with friends from the gardening club, all because they would remind Jackie of Neville. Finally, she settled on taking her mama along for the ride as she visited the recently damaged shop in Hattiesburg. Putting Mama to work resetting the store would help keep her mind off the duke.

But what would keep Diana from dwelling on Andrew?

"It wasn't supposed to work out this way," she reminded herself. "He's unemployed, unfocused, and uncommitted." One more person to look after was the last thing she needed. "Andrew and I aren't any more of a match than Mama and Neville."

But they weren't attempting to make a match. Just keeping it casual. Long-term wasn't in the forecast. They'd meet until Andrew found the right sort of woman to make heirs and spares with. Her heart ached at the thought. She paused in front of her mother's bedroom. "Be realistic, Diana. You're not Kate Middleton." She wasn't even on par with Prince Harry's American bride. "I'm a Mississippi Miss. Good at business, backwoods camping, and baking biscuits. There are no titles in your future."

Or her mother's. She plastered a smile on her face and breezed into Jackie's room. "Rise and shine, Mama. You're riding shotgun with me today."

The sight before her had her wishing she had a shotgun. The

duke was leaning over Jackie, kissing her as she slept.

"I don't know if you fancy yourself some Prince Charming type, but around here we don't take kindly to macking on unconscious women." She shoved Neville away, ready to defend her mother against his unwanted affections.

"I have you know, dear girl—"

Her mother sat up. "He wasn't—"

Andrew entered the fray. "What the bloody hell is going on here? Uncle, we have a plane to catch."

Diana jabbed a finger in Neville's direction. "Before you take Hot Lips here back to his side of the pond where he belongs, he's got some explaining to do. I caught him taking advantage of my mama while she was sleeping."

"I was most certainly not."

"I know what I saw."

Fire lit in Andrew's eyes. "Do you think my uncle is capable of doing such?"

"Di-ana Fran-ces."

Her mother's use of her full name, spit through clenched teeth stopped Diana cold. Most people had experienced the full-name treatment during childhood, but not her.

She froze in place, uncertain what to do. "Yes, ma'am?"

Jackie sat up in bed smoothing her hand over her dark hair. "Hush up and listen for once in your life. I was fully awake when you barged into my room. The duke recently left my bed and was offering me a kiss before returning to his room for fresh clothes. Had you barged in a sooner…"

Diana covered her face. "Sweet Jesus." Amid the mental image she was trying to push from her brain, a question arose. Like Andrew and her, were the older couple sharing a last moment before parting? Surely after such a spectacular fight the couple couldn't have reconciled so easily. A quick glance at Jackie's left hand confirmed, yes, indeed, those two could bounce back.

"What about what you said yesterday?"

Andrew touched her shoulder. "Let's table that for a moment. Did you think my uncle was capable of taking advantage of your mother?" His jaw ticked. "Is that the kind of family you think we are?"

For such an easygoing guy, he sure took family honor seriously. Her granddaddy would like that. "Sorry. I jumped to conclusions without having all the facts." She turned to Neville. "Your Grace, I sincerely apologize for impugning your character. I'd offer you a duel of something."

The duke waved away her offer. "Your apology is sufficient. Loving your mother as I do, I can appreciate one who's as protective towards her as you are."

"Now we have that settled, can you two please explain to me how you went from spitting nails at each other to…" She gestured to the bed, unable to say aloud what had so obviously gone on during the night.

"Couples have arguments, Diana, especially when they're

136

starting out, as the duke and I are. We're both accustomed to having things our way and that's something we'll have to work on."

"The most important thing is we're committed to making things work. It will take compromise on both our parts, but I knew from the moment I met Jackie, she'd make the perfect duchess."

A lucid response escaped her. Thankfully, Andrew had the presence of mind to ask, "So the wedding is back on?"

"It was never off, my boy."

"Diana."

What did they do now? She was fresh out of ideas. If Jackie's tirade wasn't enough to scare the man off...

"Diana."

Andrew elbowed her. "She's calling you."

"Ma'am?"

"Give me a moment to shower, and I'll meet you in the dining room for breakfast. We have a lot to accomplish in a short time." Jackie wagged her finger. "In the meantime, I suggest you and Andrew might take a moment to decide if you'll attempt another ploy to drive us apart or get onboard with this marriage."

Twenty-seven years after giving birth was a little late for Jackie to begin acting like a mother. Stunned, all Diana could manage was another, "Yes, ma'am."

Andrew tugged her out of the room. "They knew the whole time?"

"More importantly, who is that woman in there, and what did

she do with my mother?"

"I have to give you that much. She was quite a different woman than I've seen previously."

Diana reached into her jeans, finding her ever-present roll of antacids. "What do you think? Do we throw in the towel?"

The corners of his eyes crinkled. "I still have serious reservations, but I've never seen a more tenacious couple. Do you think my uncle would want to stay here in Mississippi?"

"Your guess is as good as mine. What about all those fancy parties my mama is going to have to host?"

"Bloody hell." He ran his fingers through his hair.

Diana considered offering him one of her antacids. "I'll help her as much as I can."

His eyes widened. "I don't think that will be necessary."

Well, all righty then. We've established I'll be staying on this side of the Atlantic.

She clenched her fist, a sharp response poised on her lips. Before she could sort out which orifice she wanted to shove her offer into, Andrew pulled her in tight. A quick kiss and her anger evaporated. "On the bright side, this could make things easier for us."

"There's that."

"I suppose I should cancel my flight. Again."

"Do you think they'll be happy?" she asked, when she really wondered, could she.

"To be honest, I still have my doubts about their compatibility. I've never seen two people fight and make up the way those two do. On the other hand, they seem determined."

"Were we wrong to try to keep them apart?" *Am I wrong to get involved with a man who'll only cast me aside once the appropriate British maiden appears?*

"Our intentions were good. What we did, was done out of love and concern for them."

As much as her brain warned continuing with Andrew wouldn't end with a wedding, her heart couldn't get past the pleasant present. His optimism balanced her caution. He was quick to forgive and eager to try new things. Andrew brought on her best qualities and mitigated her worst. Everyone needed a friend like him, and as for his skills as a lover—her brain could shut the heck up.

"Where does that leave us now?"

"Busy. You've got a wedding to arrange."

"I can do that in my sleep."

Andrew waggled his eyebrows. "Who says you're going to be getting any sleep."

The prospect brought heat to her cheeks. "What about you?" she asked to keep her mind above her navel. "What's on your agenda?"

"Sorting out some type of celebration for Uncle Neville."

A hundred to-dos ran through Diana's mind. Number one being slipping up to the Azalea Suite with Andrew for a few moments. But work came before fun. "All righty then. Flowers, preacher, dresses, bridal shower, and bachelor party."

"Let's get this wedding started."

In her private sitting room, Diana took the seat on the sofa next to her mama. Her brain still spun from the rapid-fire events of the morning, and more than a few questions rattled around and bobbed to the surface. A candid conversation with Andrew awaited as soon as she could slip away, but at present she and Mama had their own important topics to cover.

She opened her laptop to Greenbrier's events calendar then angled it, so Mama could see the screen. "We're booked every weekend through the summer." Taking hints had never been Jackie's strong suit, so Diana relied on a visual to support her cause.

Folding her legs beneath her, she flipped to October where they had vacant dates. "What date were you thinking for the wedding?"

Jackie took her glass of iced tea from coffee table in front of the sofa, squeezed the lemon wedge, and sipped the brew. "Sunday."

Diana faced her mama. "Which Sunday?"

"This one."

The laptop rattled to the floor. "Excuse me?"

"At three in the afternoon. That will give Pastor Beecham time to get his Sunday dinner after the morning service. It will be in the chapel instead of the larger sanctuary. I want the place to be filled with flowers and friends."

"Just a moment, please." Diana stumbled to her bathroom, a surge of acid and anxiety eating away at the lining of her stomach. "Time for the big guns." She took a long pull on a bottle of pink liquid before returning to tackle the monumental task of changing Jackie's mind.

"Wouldn't you like to wait to have a couture dress designed for you?" That could take months. While the naïve narcissists had convinced her they were truly in love, it didn't mean they shouldn't enjoy a protracted engagement.

"I'm sure The Wedding Knot has one that will do fine."

"Special order then." Diana could convince her mother's friends to host teas and showers to keep Jackie happy and busy well into the fall. "November is still warm enough to have an outdoor wedding. December would be even better. We could fill the church with poinsettias and paperwhites."

Jackie locked her jaw. Her nostrils flared. "I've said my piece and counted to three."

"Okay, Mama. Okay." Diana raised her hands in surrender. "I'll

142

make it happen. What's your color scheme?"

Bright pink spots blossomed on Jackie's cheeks. "Wonderful. First, you need to tell Mary Baxter and the other ladies from the garden club they are throwing me a shower Thursday night. I registered at Holcombe's Jewelry store downtown and of course at Sweet Tea and Lavender."

Diana snatched a notepad from the end table. From Jackie's rapid-fire instructions, it appeared making decisions wouldn't be an issue. One pitcher of sweet tea, two hours, and three full pages later, Diana had her marching orders.

Andrew settled into the little alcove where Diana and he had shared drinks the previous night. Sunlight streamed in through the bay window and glinted off the brass fixtures. Peering through the wavy glass, he took in the koi pond. Uncle Neville's romantic left turn provided the opportunity to view the water lilies Diana had described. He'd also gotten his wish to spend more time with the woman who possessed a flare for description, except it wasn't her expository skills on his brain now. The soft sounds she made in the throes of passion echoed in his mind—and the center of his chest.

He shifted in his seat and waved over the waitress. As with all things in his life, family obligations trumped personal desires. Neville would join him shortly, so they could make plans now the wedding seemed imminent.

The young woman he recalled from before approached. "What can I bring you, sir? The kitchen is still serving breakfast, or I can bring you one of Greenbrier's famous chicken salad sandwiches."

The thought of food added to the iron worry already weighing in his stomach. "No food, thank you. Tea would be nice." He quickly clarified his order, having made the mistake previously. "A pot of hot tea. Peppermint if you have it."

She nodded. "Miss Diana sent some loose-leaf over from her store so we have any flavor you like."

The waitress scurried away leaving him to appreciate her bosses' thoroughness in anticipating his preferences. She certainly didn't inherit the trait from her mother. When Uncle Neville entered, his thoughts switched from Diana's mother to his own parental figure.

Despite his capitulation, he still harbored reservations about his uncle's marriage. As he drew near, Andrew noted the man's face was as wrinkled as his shirt and trousers. "I thought you were going to change."

Neville waved his bank card in Andrew's face. "I would have, but when I went to the shop in the lobby, my bloody card wouldn't work. The clerk said it was, 'declined,' whatever that means."

It means you should have had room service launder one of the numerous outfits you've already purchased.

Andrew took the card. "Leave it to me. I'll take it up with the clerk." By that, he meant, Andrew would transfer more money into his uncle's personal account. With all the drama, he'd failed to keep the sharp eye on his family's account as he usually did.

Making a mental note to check on his parents' balances, he used the situation to address a worry featured in the snatches of sleep he'd gotten the previous night. "Have you and Jackie discussed when you'll be returning to Chatham Park?"

Andrew loved the family estate despite its crumbling brick, Edwardian plumbing, and ever-present drafts. However, it needed a great deal of work before it was ready for its latest mistress.

"Directly after the wedding. She's anxious to see her new home. I've promised her *carte blanche* to redecorate the Duchess Alexandria rooms. I can't wait for her to take up your great-grandmother's suite as well as her title."

"You did?" His voice climbed an octave. Panic washed over him. All his fears realized. Exposure, humiliation, shame. Even an obtuse woman like Jackie could add a moldering east wing to peeling paint and come up with a shoestring budget.

Thank God, the waitress returned with their tea, providing Andrew with a moment to collect his wits. After adding a spoonful of sugar, Andrew took a long sip of the soothing brew. "Did you perchance inform her she'll be walking into an apartment uninhabited for seventy years?"

With each decade, the family occupied fewer and fewer room, so that the last Duchess of Effingham, his grandmother Honoria, occupied only a modest suite adjacent to the nursery.

"It didn't come up." Neville reached for his own cup, and after

145

taking a sip peered into the liquid as if it might offer him a rescue from reality. "She wanted to talk about wedding colors."

Andrew pressed further. The time for a gentle hand had long since passed. "Have you discussed where you'll get the funds for the restoration?"

Neville's brow furrowed. "I, ah…" He scrubbed his palm over his balding pate. "I hadn't given it much thought. You've always had a head for the business side of the estate, I'm sure you'll manage the costs; you always have."

"It's not in this year's budget." Or the next. Of late, he'd had a good run in Monaco, but not nearly enough to cover restoring an entire wing.

"Well then, I'll rely on a time-tested resource—we'll ask Diana for a dowry sufficient to cover the costs."

Andrew blinked. His uncle relished all things antique, but was he serious?

"Since Jackie will be living at Chatham Park, at least part-time, I'm sure Diana wouldn't mind in the least. Nor would she want her mother living in less than ideal surroundings."

"I'm certain you're correct." Andrew would rather endure a bowl of those grits Diana kept insisting were delicious than have her learn how he earned money for the family. Or worse yet, have her think Uncle Neville had anything other than love on his heart.

Good God. What if she thought he'd pursued her for mercenary reasons?

If he flew directly from Jackson to Las Vegas and luck was truly on his side, he might have enough to do a modest restoration on the Duchess Alexandria suite. "I'd think you'd want to adequately provide for your duchess from your own coffers. As point of pride."

"You have a point." The man squared his shoulders. "It is my duty to take care of her."

Under normal circumstances, Andrew would have suggested honesty might be the best way forward. However, nothing of British aristocracy resembled normal—at least not the way his family interpreted it.

"Would you and Jackie be willing to live here for a few months. That would give me time to accrue the funds you need."

"I could take up the matter with her when we meet for lunch. She was so looking forward to meeting everyone." The corners of his mouth turned up. He leaned in and whispered, "However, I think I can persuade her I've fallen in love with Mississippi, if that will help buy you time to raise the necessary funds."

Andrew snatched the offering since it was as much help as he was likely to receive from his uncle. "Very good. That will also give you the opportunity to better prepare Jackie for her role. She'll need quite a bit of coaching before she meets Mum."

Good Lord, his mother wasn't going to relinquish her duties willingly and certainly not to a woman she thought unworthy of the job.

Neville waved away Andrew's comment. "Oh, she'll meet

Regina at the wedding."

"What?" He choked on his tea. "Mother's coming here?"

"Of course, my sister is coming to my wedding. She and your father too."

Andrew signaled their waitress and when she came within earshot, he croaked, "Whiskey. Double. Neat."

Before Diana phoned the bakery and kept a four o'clock dress fitting, she needed to find Andrew. She paused at the door to the Mimosa Suite, hoping he'd be in his new room, praying he'd be open to lending a hand, and longing to find him alone.

Maybe it would be better if he weren't.

The good Lord knew she had enough on her to-do list. Rapping lightly, she held her breath. Her knuckles had barely met oak when the door opened.

"Oh, you're here."

A sly grin spread across his face. "Were you hoping I wouldn't be?"

"I'm not sure."

"Come in and find out." He wrapped his arm around her waist and tugged her across the threshold.

"This isn't a good idea right now." Everything below her navel begged to differ. "We both have a ton of things to do in the coming days."

"All the more reason to take care of the important things first."

His kiss tasted of whiskey. Warm. Spicy. Decadent. Just like him.

"You've been drinking. Celebratory or medicinal?"

Andrew tugged her shirt free from the waist of her pants and slid his hands across her bare back. "Nothing for you to worry about."

She returned the favor, drawing Andrew's shirt over his head. As much as she'd rather spend the next week or so staring at his bare chest, worry niggled at the corners of her mind. "Easier said than done."

He scooped her into his arms, crossed to the four-poster bed, and tossed her onto it. "Our problems can keep. At least for the next half hour."

Diana shimmied out of her pants faster than a tipsy debutante would slip on a marble dance floor. "Agreed. It's not like magical elves will do the work for us."

Andrew disrobed.

Much to Diana's visual pleasure.

He joined her under the covers and made such thorough love to her, all but the most basic functions of her brain ceased.

A good hour later, Diana kissed the underside of Andrew's jaw. The world was only beginning to refocus. Her worries returning. "We do need to talk about the wedding."

"Must we?"

"You know it's in a matter of days."

"I've been told."

"I've got flowers to order, musicians to hire, and invitations to send." Was there time to mail them? God forbid they resort to emailing them.

"About that. I didn't know if Jackie gave you our guest list."

"No, I assumed—"

"My parents will be attending. They fly in Saturday."

The creases around his mouth caused a knot in her stomach. "That's fine. I'll arrange to have a car pick them up in Jackson, and there'll be room for them next door since your uncle has moved to the family quarters."

"Very good."

"What are you not telling me?"

"You have enough on your hands without concerning yourself with my relations. Leave them to me. What's my immediate task?"

Make love to me again.

All the mama-drama disappeared when they were alone. "After you reserve tuxes for you and Neville, you need to get going on a bachelor party."

"Suggestions?"

"There are several casinos in Vicksburg, and I know there are a couple guys on staff who would enjoy filling out your small numbers. Doc James for sure."

He frowned.

"If that seems a little low brow for your uncle, there's always

150

the Coach House."

"Casinos will be fine.

Did his family have a puritanical streak she didn't know about. Lordy, Mama wouldn't want to give up her Bunco games.

"I should get cracking then."

Could the twitch above his eye have something to do with his parents' arrival?

He pressed a kiss to her lips. "Text me when you get back from town."

"You bet." What wasn't he telling her? Diana tried not to borrow trouble since her little red wagon was already overflowing with issues.

Truth hit her squarely in the face. It wasn't his parents meeting Jackie worrying him. It was Diana.

Andrew closed the door to his room, cocooning Diana and him. "You look breathtaking."

She ducked her chin, reminding him of her namesake. "Oh, this old thing. It's something I pulled out of the back of the closet."

"It's not the frock I'm speaking of." If only their plans called for a quiet evening instead of separate wedding activities. He'd enjoy peeling her out of her ensemble, beginning with the stiletto heels.

"What is it then?" Diana stepped into his embrace.

"This lovely blush for one thing." He trailed his hand from her cheek, down her neck, to her décolletage. "And the way you caught the sun yesterday while lying by the pool."

"Correction. I was going over last-minute changes to the reception menu. I happened to be poolside while doing it."

"I admire the way you manage to balance work and pleasure."

He appreciated everything about her, especially the way their bodies fit so nicely together.

"Too bad we can't do a better job of creating that equilibrium tonight. What time do you think you and the guys will be back from Vicksburg?"

"Uncle Neville likes to stick to his schedule. Dinner at eight. Bed by eleven."

"Mama's bridal shower will be over long before then."

Andrew fingered a curl that had come lose from her chignon. "Will you wait up for me?"

"I could be persuaded to forfeit sleep for the right price."

He nibbled her earlobe. "I have the offering in mind."

"You have a deal." She kissed the underside of his jaw. "Room service will bring you up something as soon as you return."

He'd come to love Greenbrier's *room service*. "Now you're making it difficult for me to leave."

She tugged from his embrace. "I know. Me too."

"If we're going to keep things under wraps, we need to be careful." Guilt panged him. Nothing in the world would give him greater pleasure than to tell the whole world he'd fallen for Diana Curtis. However, in revealing the fact, he'd risk exposing another. One he was desperate to keep from her. "We wouldn't want to take focus away from Neville and Jackie's happy event."

Diana gnawed her lip. "You're right." She lowered her gaze. "I'll see you later. Have a good time with Doc James and the guys."

He barked a laugh. "I'm sure it will be a night to remember."

Greenbrier's chef, the head gardener, and the husband of Diana's events manager were joining the veterinarian for Neville's bachelor party. As pleasant as the chaps surely were, he barely knew them, and the only thing they had in common were the Curtis women—not much to base an entire evening's conversation on. Especially when he suspected Doc James harbored feelings for Diana.

Not long after slipping from Andrew's suite, Diana sat in a metal folding chair Mrs. Baxter had borrowed from the church hall. Along with the other women in the living room, she balanced a plate of cheese straws and petit fours on her knee while attempting to drink the ubiquitous, frothy punch.

At least it's lime sherbet this time.

Diana sipped the syrupy-sweet concoction as her mother opened presents. Between nibbles, she recorded the gifts and the giver, so Jackie could get started on the thank-you notes first thing in the morning. Her mind wandered beyond the place settings and dish towels. It wasn't the dress-ruining raspberry punch from the last wedding hosted at Greenbrier on her mind now.

What was Andrew's secret?

She'd known him a matter of days, so inevitably there were mountains of undivulged facts. Habits, preferences, girlfriends. This was bigger, deeper, broader. And he was actively keeping it from her.

"You're looking tired, dear. Have you been working too hard?" Diana's kindergarten teacher studied her with the same critical eye as when she'd colored pictures outside the lines.

Diana smiled at the well-preserved matron on her right. "Not too hard, Mrs. Leffler. Just the right amount."

Only planning a wedding fit for the queen of the garden club in less than a week all while maintaining two other enterprises.

"Have you considered adding an eye cream to your nightly routine. It's never too early to fight Father Time." Since retiring, the woman had begun selling Mary Maybelle Cosmetics and earned a lilac convertible for her efforts.

"I'll borrow Mama's."

"When can we expect to hear wedding bells for you?"

"Not any time soon. I'm married to my work at present."

Diana looked around the room. Much had changed in their little corner of the world in the space of a generation. Among the attendees were an optometrist, school administrator, police officer, and several business owners mixed in with the stay-at-home moms. Rather than easing the pressure to adhere to traditional gender roles, it seemed to add to societal expectations. Now a woman had to do it all, have it all, be it all, to be considered a success. Right now, she would settle for keeping her accounts in the black and a corner piece of Beverly Bakery's famous sheet cake with cream cheese frosting.

A future with Andrew seemed too much to expect.

Her thoughts raced ahead to Lord and Lady Somerset's arrival tomorrow. Dread snaked up her spine and not only because they were laying eyes on the next Duchess of Effingham for the first time.

Having only dated guys from Greenville, she'd never experienced a meet-the-parents moment. They'd all known her since birth. What would Andrew's folks think of her? Not that it mattered, since they wouldn't be meeting her as Andrew's love interest. Still…

From her left, Jasmine elbowed her. "Pay attention. You're supposed to be writing this down."

Diana jolted. "Right." She tracked the movement of presents as they circled the room. "What did I miss?"

"Only Ida Douglas's gift."

Purple. Crocheted. Placemats. "Oh my."

"Wonder how that's going to look in Dukie Dear's castle."

Diana stifled a laugh. "Stop. It's bad enough when Mama says it. Besides I don't think Chatham Park is a castle."

"Have you seen pictures?"

"Only on the internet. It's big though. Makes Greenbrier look like a doublewide."

The day Neville and Andrew arrived, Diana did a basic search on the aristocrats. Burke's Peerage, Debrett's, and good ole Wikipedia. The snooping shamed her now she knew them better. At the time she wanted to make certain whom her mother had dragged home.

"Have they said when they're leaving?"

"Not for a while. Andrew suggested they stay here for a few months." Which had set off alarm bells. Why didn't he want the newlyweds in England? That paired with her questions regarding his need to keep their relationship under wraps. Her lover was keeping secrets, but what, she couldn't figure out.

Between that and making love with said secret-keeper, no wonder Mrs. Leffler suggested eye cream. Before things returned to normal she'd probably be the woman's best customer.

Ten miles south of Greenville, in the moderately larger metropolis of Vicksburg, Andrew, Neville and their motley crew of revelers were in their second stop of the night—a private dining room of a casino.

"Talk about a busman's holiday."

The rattle of electronic gaming machines permeated through the red, flocked walls. Of all the gaming establishments he'd frequented in his career, the Lucky Lady had to be the most neon saturated. Even their dining table boasted a rope of flashing blue glowing beneath.

"A toast," Doc James raised his voice as well as his glass. "To the groom. Many happy years ahead."

Chef eyed Uncle Neville over his pint. "You be good to Miss Jackie."

Greenbrier's gardener grinned. "Hear, hear." Despite getting carded at every turn, he seemed to be enjoying the stag night—perhaps better than all the others combined. He took another sip of his beer then wiped the foam from his lips. "She's one of a kind."

Jasmine's husband, an army sergeant called Wes, added his voice. "We love her like our own mother."

Uncle Neville tipped his glass of whiskey to each man in turn. "I shall endeavor to make her the happiest woman alive."

"One of us ought to give the duke some words of wisdom," said the sergeant. "Isn't that part of what we're supposed to be doing tonight? At least that's what Jasmine told me."

"I'm out." Young Jacob raised his hands in surrender. "I'm on the lifetime bachelor plan."

"How about you, Sarge?" Chef asked. "You and Jasmine have a good thing going. Let's hear something from you."

"She's put up with me through five deployments. I'm lucky to have her, and she makes sure I know it."

Chef jabbed Wes in the shoulder with a beefy finger. "Come on, there has to be something."

He ran his palm over his close-cropped afro. "I bring her coffee in bed every morning."

Andrew made eye contact with Neville across the table.

Don't say it. Don't say a word about staff bringing breakfast to the estate's chatelaine *in her suite.*

"Sounds like a wise practice. I'll remember that one."

Andrew let out a breath and quickly shifted the focus. "How about you, Doc? You've been awfully quiet tonight."

"Like that's unusual," Jacob muttered.

"I don't have anything to offer on the matter."

"Yeah, we all know the only females you're interested in have four legs and eat grass."

He laughed. "They are easier to decipher than the two-legged variety."

"Now I happen to know you went out with Khristy Williams a few years back," Wes said.

"And you've had a thing for Miss Diana as long as I've know you," Jacob added.

Andrew's hackles rose. Which was ridiculous. He could hardly blame the chap for admiring Diana. Wanting to be with her. Only an idiot wouldn't. Or die trying to find a way to make himself worthy of her.

"The only advice I've got is to never keep secrets nor let something small or insignificant stand in the way of love. Especially not something stupid like pride."

Wes nodded. "The Good Book does say it goeth before a fall."

Andrew disagreed with this bit of advice. What would Diana think of his family—of him—if she knew. And pride, when it was all one had, one clung to it quite tightly. His gaze shot to his uncle who was taking in the marital advice with the solemnity of the marriage vows he'd take in a few days. Pride and duty kept Andrew going when he wanted to call it a day. Wanted to go his own way. Wanted…Diana.

He clapped his hands, shaking them all from their gravity. "Now we have the serious business out of the way, it's on to the fun."

"This isn't a topless show." Wes' black eyes widened. "I

promised Jasmine the only boobies I'd ever look at are hers."

"Hen-pecked, much?" Jacob taunted from across the table.

"Gladly. You've seen my wife?"

"No need to worry. It's a family-friendly show." Andrew had arranged for them to see a well-known troupe who employed drums and paint as their means of entertainment. Their seats were center-front but out of the splash-zone. "We better head in so we're not late."

The men had settled in their seats and the house lights lowered when his phone vibrated in his pocket. His first impulse was to ignore it, but with his parents soon in route, he dared not.

Maybe it's Diana texting that she's waiting for me.

No such luck.

—Bank of England. Overdraft alert. Account ending in 5743 is overdrawn by £2,374.67—

Acid churned in his stomach. His father's account. As if he didn't have enough to manage with Uncle Neville. What was his old man up to now? There was nothing for it but to cover the overdraft—plus a bit more. Problem was, having been away from his work his own coffers were less than he liked. As it so happened a source of income lay yards away. He leaned over to his uncle. "I have a matter needing my attention."

Neville arched a brow. "Problem?"

"Nothing I can't handle with a little time at the tables."

"Anything I can do?"

"Possibly." They'd ridden together in the sergeant's large SUV.

"I'll need to stay if the table is hot." Which could jeopardize his date with Diana. Bloody hell, he'd grown weary of this rock-and-hard-place.

"I'll need to delay our departure without drawing attention to the reason why."

"If you can manage it."

"Count on me. I can suggest a round of drinks or time at the slot machines."

Andrew gripped Neville's shoulder as he rose from his seat. "Wish me luck."

After exiting the theater, he wound his way through the main lobby, past the areas where poker and roulette were played, and over to the blackjack tables. He motioned a waitress for a drink and took his time surveying the ongoing games while he waited. Hot tables were to be avoided. Too much attention for his purposes. Tables with too many available seats didn't suit either for the same reason. By the time his gin and tonic arrived, he'd found what he wanted. A couple of tourists mixed with university-aged students and an older man. Most importantly, the dealer had started a new shoe.

He settled in the seat on the far left and placed the minimum bet. His gaze found the security cameras and the pit boss. The dealer dealt everyone's cards, giving Andrew a ten of clubs and seven of diamonds.

The man to his right leaned over. "You're going to want to hold on that one."

Andrew often received advice from fellow players. Some gave it to steer others wrong. Some because it made them feel like a whale. Some were lonely and wanted to talk.

This man appeared to fall in the last category. Dressed in a leisure suit straight out of the seventies with a hairstyle to match, it seemed possible he'd been in residence since that decade.

"I believe I'll take that advice." After all, Andrew liked to begin conservatively until the shoe swung in favor of the players.

More cards were drawn. The tourists busted. And when the dealer drew a nine of spades to his collective seventeen, he also went over twenty-one. Andrew and the old pro collected their winnings while the dealer cleared the cards.

Andrew raised his gin and tonic. "Cheers."

"Dusty," the man said offering his hand.

"Andrew." He signaled the waitress. "A drink for my friend. What's your pleasure?"

"These days I stick to Cokes. It helps with the concentration."

Another round began with bets placed and cards dealt.

"More sage wisdom." Between keeping track of the count, his strategy, and the pit boss's location, he had plenty to fill his brain. Add an awareness of time, financial pressure, and a simmering desire for the end of the evening and smoke should have been coming out his ears.

Several hands passed with Andrew splitting his bets when appropriate, steadily increasing his wager, and only busting once. The other players made small talk with Andrew and Dusty keeping to themselves.

"Card," he said, calculating the next would likely be a low one. It was. Which brought Andrew's winnings up to a thousand. On the next hand, along with his bet he added a tip for the dealer.

Dusty polished off his Coke. "You're not from around here, are you?"

"I'm based in London. You?"

A dozen hands passed in silence. The table got hotter and despite the pit boss replacing the dealer, Andrew continued to play his strategy and win.

"I used to live in a town not too far up the road."

The old gambler had been silent for so long, Andrew had trouble recalling the thread of their conversation. "What's the name?"

"You wouldn't have heard of it. It's barely bigger than a gnat's ass. Greenville. Born, bred, and wed. Haven't been back for more than twenty years though. Not sure what calls me back to this part of the country now."

"I've heard of it. My uncle and I are staying at the Greenbrier."

"You know the owner, old man Dansfield?"

"He's deceased. A few years ago, from what I've been told. I'm acquainted with his granddaughter, Miss Diana Curtis."

Dusty's gaze narrowed. "I 'spect you are."

The hairs on Andrew's arm stood at attention. "Lovely lady. Good head on her shoulders." He'd made enough to cover his immediate problem. "I'm going to cash in. My uncle and I are out celebrating his stag night, and I've already been away from the group too long."

"Who's your uncle marrying? It might be someone I used to know."

"Diana's mother, Jackie."

The gambler stiffened for the briefest moment. "That a fact?" He turned his attention to his hand. "Enjoy your night."

Bloody hell. If only he could snatch back his words. Have chosen another table. "We will."

Andrew collected his winnings, hurrying to the lobby where he found Uncle Neville and the others waiting. There'd been moments when he'd left a casino—with help. There were establishments that would no longer book his action. However, he'd never left with the feeling a problem would follow him—until now.

With the wedding rehearsal later that day, Diana hurried out of her office. As always balancing the needs of her two dependents—her businesses and her mama.

Rose petals, green ribbon, groom's gift, Yeti coolers, SEC tumblers, buy advertising for Greenbrier in the Mobile newspaper.

In the narrow service hallway, she nearly collided with the duke as he exited the kitchen. *Carrying a breakfast tray?*

"Good morning, Your Grace."

I didn't know he knew where food came from, much less could ferret out its source.

"Please, call me Neville. Now we're to be family, I think we can dispense with the formalities."

She pointed to the tray containing a carafe, toast, and two poached eggs. "I hope my staff has been taking care of your needs."

"Most certainly. I wanted to bring your mother her breakfast myself. A bit of advice I received from one of the gentlemen during my stag night."

The gesture screamed Wes and Jasmine. After her grandparents, those two best exemplified a healthy, loving marriage. "That's so kind. I'm sure Mama will be thrilled."

"I must be on my way. Cold eggs won't do."

As he turned, she gave voice to the question muddling her mental to-do list. "Duk— I mean, Neville, do you happen to know where Andrew is?"

"Did you need him for a task?"

"Not exactly. I hadn't seen him around lately." Prior to the stag night, he'd been her constant companion. Friday, he'd briefly stopped by her office before disappearing for the day.

Neville studied the floor. "I have him taking care of last-minute wedding things. I believe it's the American custom for the groom's family to host a dinner following the wedding rehearsal."

"We call it a rehearsal dinner."

"I've made arrangements with your staff to use the breakfast room. It should suffice for our small numbers."

"I assume Andrew's parents will attend." Another detail to manage. Would they want one room or two?

"Lord and Lady Somerset will round out our numbers to an even dozen. Counting the page and bridesmaid."

One of Granddaddy Dansfield's favorite sayings tickled her ear.

A pound of pretention is worth a pound of manure. She stifled a snicker and wondered if she'd ever get used to all the British terms Neville used for ordinary things like ring bearer and flower girl. "I have everything ready for their arrival."

"I'm sure you do. I much admire your efficiency." His gaze softened. "And your dedication to your mother, despite the shenanigans you and Andrew attempted. You're a credit to your family. Just as he is to mine."

"That's kind of you to say." Despite her growing to-do list, she wanted to keep him talking, especially if he was in the mood to be frank. "Do you mind, Neville, if I ask you a personal question?"

"You may ask, but I may not answer. Talking about my private life is against my upbringing as well as my nature."

"I wondered why you hadn't married before now. Being as it's so important to your position to produce an heir."

He raised his chin. "I hadn't met your mother yet."

Not the straight answer she'd hoped for, though her mama would be thrilled with the romantic notion. "I see. Thank you."

"There's also a more truthful reason if you'd like to hear it."

His words stilled her steps. "If it's not prying too much."

"Andrew is like a son to me. Has been since he was a little chap in knee pants. I don't imagine my own progeny could be dearer to my heart. Simply said, I wouldn't do anything to displace him as the heir to my title."

The urge to hug the man struck her. "That's touching. I know he feels the same about you."

"If I speak to Andrew during the day, should I tell him to seek you out?"

"Please. If I'm not in my office, he can find me in the barn."

He turned from her. "Very well, and now I must tend to your mother."

At the service entrance, Diana changed into boots before heading down to the barn. She and her mother still needed to finalize the reception seating chart, and there was a snafu regarding an order of Vera Bradley purses for Sweet Tea and Lavender. When there was a foal in the barn, work took a back seat. At least for a few minutes.

Stepping out of the sunlight, her vision took a moment to adjust to the barn's shadows. When it did, the large blur at the far end turned into Doc James and his gelding.

"Morning." She closed the gap between them. "Did you see Hope's baby?"

He lowered the hoof he'd been cleaning and took up a curry comb. "I took a quick look before Toby and I hit the trails. He's looking good."

"Thank you again for joining the bachelor party. I know that's not your thing."

"We had a good time. The duke is…"

"Stuffy, peculiar, and a bit of a dandy."

He nodded. "And a good fit for Miss Jackie."

She ran her hand along the horse's warm flank. "He's certainly

170

devoted to her. I ran into him a little while ago, and he was bringing breakfast to Mama."

"That's on advice from Wes."

"I hope it works. They had another argument at dinner last night." Good Lord, what would she do if they cancelled the wedding now?

The vet dropped the circular comb into the bucket at his feet then turned to face her. "I'm glad you came down here." He shoved his hands in his pockets. Shifted his weight from foot-to-foot. Grabbed the grooming kit and moved it to the wall next to Toby's stall.

All the while her heart beat double time. Why couldn't he have asked her out a couple weeks ago when dukes, lords, and especially a certain viscount were only in little girls' dreams. Finally, her impatience got the better of her. "Something on your mind?"

James removed his Stetson, knocking the trail dust off against his thigh. "One thing about our night in Vicksburg struck me as strange. I've been stewing about whether to mention it. I'd decided not to, but seeing as you're here, and you and I are thinking along the same lines, I better."

Not asking her out. But still, as he hemmed and hawed, she wanted to take him by the shoulders and shake it out of him. Even Toby showed his impatience, stamping his hoof against the stable's concrete floor. "Do I need to be sitting down for this?"

"No, it's a small thing, when you think about it."

"Let's hear it. My imagination's working overtime here."

"As the show was about to start, Andrew left. And didn't come back."

Just as he'd disappeared all day Friday, not returning until after supper time. "That's not polite, and not like him. Wonder where he went."

James met her gaze. "The blackjack tables. I had to take a call about Mrs. Meriwether's dog. It's got arthritis and she worries. Afterward, the ushers held me off until intermission. I took to wandering and found him."

Strange, but not enough to warrant a mention. Perhaps the same had happened to him.

"Here's the thing, he was winning big time. Nearly every hand."

She failed to see the point. "He's one of idle rich. I guess that's what they do when they're bored."

"All day?" James' voice rose. "I had to go through Vicksburg yesterday morning on the way to a cattle auction. My route took me past the Lucky Lady. One of Greenbrier's vehicles parked out front."

The same vehicle Andrew had borrowed. He'd turned down her offer of a picnic to gamble. He'd *lied.* Told her he needed to take care of an issue with Neville's tuxedo.

He shrugged. "It was still there when I came back through at four o'clock."

Diana's temper flared. She bet her shoe money it was parked there at this moment. What. The. Hell. Was middle-class America boring him?

"It feels wrong telling you. None of my business what your guests do. But it seemed more wrong not to let you know."

"You did the right thing. I appreciate your concern for me and Mama."

James toed the ground. "Anyway."

Was he blushing? Good Lord, most men with such good looks would be crowing like a rooster.

He unhooked Toby's halter, letting the animal take himself out to pasture. "I better get to going. I've got cows to castrate over at Brawner's farm." Leaving her with that mental image, James ambled to his truck.

"All Andrew had to do was say he wanted to visit the Lucky Lady again. It's not like he's accountable to me for his time." So why the deceit? Her palm tingled, making her think she'd had the right idea about him back at the airport. What irritated like a pebble in her shoe was his lack of candor. "Silly me for thinking this was more than a diversion." One he could easily replace with a set of cards.

She moved down to Hope's stall. For all her years, her home brought her the only solace she needed. Now, watching the two-day-old colt failed. "I think I've earned a few days in Biloxi after this is over. Maybe an ocean view is what I need." The quarter horse snorted a reply. "Yeah, I know. Fat chance of me getting away."

The sound of Greenbrier's van rattling up the driveway had her pulse doing double time. For moment she considered hiding in the tack room—at least until she got her temper out of the red zone.

"Neville said you were looking for me."

Diana drew in a breath and prayed for self-control. She tucked her hands in her pockets for good measure. His dark hair blew in the breeze and whiskers shadowed his jaw. The memory of them against her cheek had different parts of her tingling now. Damn his good looks. Now she needed a different type of self-control. "Just curious if there was anything you wanted me to do for the rehearsal dinner tonight."

He closed the distance between them. "It's all handled." His blue eyes danced, and his face shone like she hadn't seen since their first real kiss back when he found her in the woods.

As he reached for her she sidestepped him by picking up the bucket of grooming tools Doc James left and hugging it. "Special instructions for your folks?" She'd had her fill of loving a liar when she was dating Travis.

His smile faltered. "Just be your usual charming self."

"It's not me I'm worried about," she said, moving them to safer territory. If they kept to wedding issues, all would be well. "I can't help thinking our mothers are going to get along like two cats with their tails tied together."

"I understand your concerns, and I wish I could say they were baseless."

"Is this why you suggested Neville and Mama live here for a while? To give your mother time to adjust to no longer being your uncle's hostess?"

His jaw ticked—a movement so small she wouldn't have seen it had she not been watching him intently. "I thought it would be a good idea for the newlyweds to adjust to married life here where they enjoy so much support."

"You have a point." But her gut screamed that wasn't the only reason.

Andrew took the bucket, setting it on the ground. "We have an hour before my parents arrive." He wrapped his arms around her. "How about we make the most of it?"

His kisses tested her resolve. "Some of us have to work." She broke from his embrace.

He followed behind her. "Want company?"

She sped up, leaving him standing by the side of the barn. "I've got maid-of-honor duties to attend to, and I'm certain you can find ways of keeping yourself occupied."

From heaven's heights Grandma Dansfield clucked her tongue and scolded. *Girl, where are your manners?*

Better rude than a fool. The good Lord above knew another second of him playing with her hair and she'd be dragging him up to the hayloft. "Twenty-four hours. This time tomorrow Mama will be married off, and this whole ordeal will be over."

16

Pride kept Andrew rooted to the ground for several minutes after Diana disappeared into the mansion. Tension coiled in his belly. Fear of losing her completely got his feet moving. At the gate where thick grass met the formal gardens, he paused.

Find Diana. Explain. Make her understand.

Doing so required a level of candor he wasn't yet prepared to offer. More weeks like today, and she need never know how few digits his bank account contained. Uncle Neville could offer his bride a beautiful home. His parents could continue in the style they were accustomed. He could face Diana as one worthy of her. Until then, he had to keep her from giving up on him.

Taking the crushed-shell path around to Greenbrier's front, he spent a good hour in one of the large rockers on the mansion's porch, rehearsing the toast he'd give that evening—as well as the warning he'd offer his parents. Be polite to Diana and Jackie *or else*.

With his speeches perfected, Andrew meant to return to his suite to wait for his parents' arrival. He planted a foot on the curved staircase's bottom tread. The mahogany protested his weight, echoing the discord between his head and his heart. "A quick word with her." He reversed course, taking the long hallway to the back of the mansion. "That's all."

At her office door, he paused. "I'll simply ask her to be patient a little while." He rapped against the oak. "Please be in there. Alone. And happy to see me again."

"What is it now?"

So much for the receptive mood.

Andrew cracked the door and stuck his head inside. "It's me. Can we talk for a moment before my parents arrive?"

She waved him in. "Might as well. Everyone else has paraded through here."

"I'll be brief. Based on my reception in the barn, I'm guessing the veterinarian has relayed details about Neville's stag night."

She steepled her fingers. "He's looking out for my family's welfare."

"I respect that." He closed the door to her office then walked to the edge of her desk where he rested his hip. "I want to allay any fears you might have about my gambling." He caught her gaze. "I do not have an addiction. It's simply a diversion."

Diana leaned back, crossing her arms. "That's what I explained to him."

Andrew shuttered his eyes. *She believes my lie.*

"You're accustomed to spending your time differently than we do."

His stomach knotted. Never had he pursued a woman to this degree. Never had to. Never wanted to. "Speaking of time, I'd very much like to spend some of it with you after the wedding." He paused, waiting for a reaction. So far, her body language suggested her patience with him was thin.

She pursed her lips. "Really?"

He captured her hand. "Could I interest you in escaping to the beach?" A few glorious days where he could finally concentrate solely on her.

"What would we tell people?"

"I don't see why we would have to say anything. Neville and Jackie are headed to Natchez for their riverboat-cruise honeymoon. You can surely leave Jasmine in charge and take a day or two off. And no one here will wonder where I've gone."

"I was thinking about heading down to Biloxi." Her expression softened. "Walks on the beach would do me good."

"Sounds lovely."

"Trust me, it will be."

Nothing would give Diana greater pleasure. Except for maybe to have him rub suntan oil on her while they sipped drinks on the beach. "Okay. I'll trust you." She snagged her phone from her desk, swiping the screen to reveal the time. "Your parents are ten minutes out, so I need to get cracking." She opened the staff's group text and sounded battle-stations. "I've got to pry Mama away from the mirror and grab the bouquet from the fridge. Jasmine's youngest, Starr, is doing the presentation."

"Are you giving my parents a formal reception?"

She shrugged. "You never get a second chance to make a first impression." Slipping her phone into the pocket of her dress, she crossed the room. "I'm channeling *Downton Abbey*. All the staff and I are going to greet your parents at Greenbrier's entrance."

Andrew followed her into the hall. "That's perfect. My mother will be thrilled. She loves being the center of attention."

"Curtsey, yes or no?"

"You'll have her eating out of the palm of your hand."

"Excellent." With Andrew in tow, she sidetracked to the family quarters, finding them empty. "I want to make this as easy for Mama and Neville as possible."

They walked the length of the mansion to the reception area. "You're on board with this marriage?"

"Aren't you?"

He shrugged. "When I'm in, I'm in."

Diana caught the sound of tires against stone. "It looks like it's show time either way." She hastened her steps, opening Greenbrier's etched-glass doors as Billy parked their newest SUV between the two iron planters flanking the entrance.

As she'd asked, the staff were lined up and ready to impress in Greenbrier's signature dark purple polos and pressed khakis. She slipped in line next to Jasmine, instead of joining Andrew, Neville, and Jackie on the porch. Today was Mama's day to play hostess. Her day to shine.

Jackie's hands flapped at her side as Lord and Lady Somerset alighted from the car. From across the way, Diana willed calm to her mama.

Steady. Like we practiced.

The staff bobbed and bowed. Starr, dressed in her Easter finery, presented her ladyship with a bouquet of flowers freshly cut from the garden. The high-born guests smiled their appreciation.

Then Jackie broke rank. Tottering on a brand-new pair of Louboutins she'd gotten on a trip to Atlanta, she caught her future sister-in-law in a fierce hug. "I'm tickled to meet you, Regina. I know we're going to be best friends."

"She's gone rogue," Chef muttered—loudly enough for Diana to hear from the other end of the line.

"I thought she was supposed to wait until—" Jasmine added.

"She was." Diana popped an antacid.

Jackie moved on to her next victim, opening her arms and stepping toward Andrew's father.

He thrust out his hand, having had time to prepare for Jackie's preferred method of greeting. "Pleasure to meet you, Mrs. Curtis."

Not one to be thwarted, Jackie managed a handshake/cheek kiss combo that turned the mans' face florid. "Cecil, I hope you've brought your appetite with you. We've been cooking pig meat since the butt-crack of dawn this morning. As soon as we get done with the rehearsal, we'll be tying on the feed bag."

After Jackie's exuberant welcome, the aristocratic couple stood frozen in place. Like two calves after their first experience with an electric fence. Of the scene's audience, Andrew recovered first. He pressed a light kiss to his mother's cheek before extending his hand to his father. "I'd like you to meet Jackie's daughter." He motioned for her to join them.

This wasn't the plan. *At all.*

The pair turned their judgie stares her way.

She'd hoped to delay facing Andrew's mama and daddy if possible. Her knees knocked. A flashback of an ill-fated, pre-teen, pastor-mandated rendition of "Jesus Wants Me for a Sunbeam" hit her hard.

After Mama's wild greeting, Diana had a lot of decorum to make up for. Then again, if she didn't faint, throw up, or sing off key she could hardly do worse. She drew near but stayed an arm's length from the new arrivals who'd yet to recover from their initial brush with southern hospitality.

Andrew tugged her closer to his parents. His blue gaze warmed her from the inside out. "Mother, Father, I'd like to introduce Miss Diana Curtis."

They braced for impact.

No, you're not about to get another hug.

"Diana, please meet my parents, Lord and Lady Somerset."

She kept her hands by her side and a smile plastered on her face. The protocol standoff continued for several heartbeats before she caved. "A pleasure to meet you both." She gestured toward the front door, eliciting a flinch from both guests. "Let's get you out of this heat."

Diana took two steps then turned to see if anyone was following her. "After you settle in, my staff has prepared our version of afternoon tea for your refreshment."

They huddled together like lost children until they reached the porch. There their eyes widened, necks craned, and demeanors changed as they stepped into the wide foyer. The lead glass doors, grand staircase, and oak paneling never failed to impress. Lady Somerset finally found her voice. "You have a lovely home, Jackie." Her clipped accent's sharp edges screamed of begrudging appreciation.

"I have to give credit where it's due. Diana's the one responsible for restoring our home to its former glory." She locked arms with Neville. "And ensuring Dukie Dear and I never have to worry about anything but how long to stay in each other's country."

"Is that so?" Lord Somerset's eyes might have been the same

shade of blue, but they held none of the warmth of his son's. "You must tell me more." As they narrowed on her they also reminded her of a turkey buzzard circling roadkill.

"Certainly, Your Lordship. Over my special spiked lemonade and pimento cheese sandwiches."

Following the rehearsal, Andrew rode beside Diana as she drove his parents back from the church. Except for a few whispered remarks, his mother had remained largely silent. She need not voice her opinion since it radiated from her stiff carriage. On the other hand, his father delighted in Jackie's little jokes, praised Greenbrier's beauty, and hung on Diana's every word.

Cecil leaned forward to ask, "What other enterprises have you undertaken, besides your shop and the B&B?"

"I purchased two hundred acres recently and plan to turn it into a hunting lodge."

"And it seems everything you touch turns to gold, my dear."

"After a great deal of hard work," Andrew added.

She shot him a smile. "Which I keep telling you isn't a bad thing."

At the mansion's entrance, Diana stopped the 4x4, everyone exited, and a staff member drove the vehicle off. Once in the foyer Diana motioned them into the empty bar. "Please make yourselves comfortable. I'm going to see if they're ready for us in the breakfast room."

Her magnificent backside had slipped from view when his parents dropped their pretense. Like marionettes with their strings cut, they flopped into a pair of club chairs and let out twin sighs.

Cecil fanned himself with a magazine he picked up from the cocktail table. "It's hotter than Cannes in July."

Regina cut her eyes at Andrew. "Not that we've holidayed there recently."

Twenty-four hours and this will all be over.

Andrew clung to the promise and the prospect of viewing Diana's bikini clad body. "Jackie says the humidity is good for the complexion."

"Spare me any more of that woman's colloquialisms."

"Be nice, Mother. She makes Uncle Neville happy."

"I can't imagine how. She's thick as a plank."

"If you can't be nice, keep silent. For some reason, the Curtis women believe British aristocracy equates to good manners. I'd like to keep them thinking so." He also wanted Diana to believe he was a man of character, who deserved her. And he was willing to do whatever it took to make it so.

His father cleared his throat. "A word." He nodded toward the far corner of the bar. "In private."

"I can't give you more money this month, Father." Andrew caught his mother's gaze, to include her in the conversation. "You're going to have to learn to economize."

"Not if you listen to me I won't." Cecil leaned forward and

lowered his voice. "I think it's high time you marry."

"I've heard this speech before. I understand your expectations. I'm to marry a titled girl whose father can bestow upon her enough money to set Chatham Park right and take care of you and Mother."

"Perhaps I've been too narrowminded. I think a more modern approach would be better."

Andrew's hackles stood to attention. "No." He'd seen the calculating looks his parents shared.

"Hear me out." Cecil pounded the table. "Diana is perfect. Absolutely everything we could hope for."

Diana had intended to wait until Andrew and his parents finished their conversation before announcing dinner was ready. Until she caught her name on Lord Somerset's lips. Curiosity had her edging as close to the open doorway as she dared.

"I wouldn't consider it." Andrew's voice rose to match his father's.

She stumbled back as she processed the topic of conversation. *Her.* And Lord Somerset's view she and Andrew would make a good marriage.

"Every time I think you couldn't shock me, Father, you prove me wrong."

No one ever hears anything pleasing when they eavesdrop.

But they often learned the truth.

In her heart she'd always known, but there was nothing like having it spelled out. She dashed angry tears away. "Stupid fool. How many times has he told me the type of woman he would marry?" One who made Duchess Kate seem common. Her stomach heaved at the imagery her brain conjured up of Andrew's future bride and her naivete for believing his empty promises.

Well, Viscount Snobby Pants had another thing coming if he thought she was slinking off to Biloxi with him.

A conversation for after Mama's wedding. That's what mattered now. She'd see to it Jackie and Neville's wedding went off without a hitch. Then she and Andrew would have their come-to-Jesus meeting.

Diana dried her eyes, straightened her spine, and plastered on a smile. She tapped on the doorframe. "Lord and Lady Somerset, Andrew, we're serving dinner."

Andrew's parents swanned off down the hall, and as she moved to follow, he caught her arm. "We need to talk."

He tried to wrap an arm around her, but she managed to wiggle from his grasp. "You bet your boots we do, but now's not the time for what I need to say to you." She needed plenty of room for the fur that would fly when she finally got to cut loose on him.

Andrew pulled them into the library. "Here. Now." He took her in his arms, holding her tight.

She fought against him. "Damn you, Andrew Montgomery. Let me go or I'll make that slap I gave you look like a love tap."

"You overheard my father and me, didn't you?"

She kicked up her chin. "My ears were certainly burning."

He took her hands in his. "Let me explain."

"I think I understand well enough. I know what I heard."

Jackie burst into the room. "What are you two doing out here? Soup's getting cold."

Diana turned her frustrations on her mama. "It's vichyssoise. It's already cold."

Mama snapped her fingers. "Get in here." Her words came out as a hiss. "Lady Somerset is fit to be tied."

"Fine." She turned to Andrew. "After Mama and Neville's wedding, I'll give you exactly five minutes to explain why I shouldn't run you out of town on a rail."

Mama's wedding day arrived to the wail of the weather siren. Outside the family quarters, strong winds upturned the patio umbrellas. Fat raindrops pummeled every blossom in the garden. Lightning scrapped plans for a carriage ride to the church.

"We have a short window between storms coming up. You good to go yet, Mama?"

Jackie hummed "Here Comes the Bride" as the hairdresser from Patsy's Hair Castle pinned a short veil to her dark tresses. In deference to her second-go-around bride status, she'd selected a tea-length dress with an ivory lace overlay and a scooped neckline. Later she'd carry a nosegay of pale pink roses, saved from the storm in the nick of time.

"Ta-da." Patsy hit the bride with a final flourish of hairspray. "Isn't she pretty?"

Diana smiled. "Don't think I've ever seen a lovelier bride."

The living room's other occupants, Jasmine, Starr, and Wes Jr., voiced their agreement.

Jackie beamed. "Y'all are precious to say so. I think we all make a magazine-worthy bridal party." She straightened the bow on her flower girl's dress, offered the ring bearer two thumbs up, and lasered her focus on Diana. "Let's see what we can do about those dark circles. Why haven't you been using the eye cream you borrowed? You look like something the cat killed then drug through hedgerow backwards."

No amount of eye cream could repair what an all-night crying jag had done. She'd replayed Andrew's words with his father over and over, analyzed every nuance of their conversation, without drawing any conclusion other than the one she drawn in the library. Andrew only saw her as a woman-of-the-moment until her could find the lady-for-life.

She waved away her mama's concern. "No one's going to be looking at me today. Not with you around."

"I don't know." Jackie puffed the capped sleeve on Diana's drop-waist dress. "This complements your fair skin wonderfully."

"Thanks for choosing the jade-colored one." With the vacant spot on the color spectrum filled, she could add a line of resale bridesmaid dresses to Sweet Tea and Lavender's products.

The rumbles of thunder grew further apart, less window shaking. Diana checked the weather app on her phone. "This is it. Let's go." She turned to Jasmine. "Text Billy to pull the car as close to the back door as possible."

A rap on the door stopped her from issuing the rest of her orders. Regina stuck her head in the door. "Mind if I have a quick word with the bride?"

"Please, come in." Jackie's wide gaze bounced from the new arrival to the room's other adults. They shrugged their reply.

"Doesn't everyone look colorful in their wedding finery." Lady Somerset herself wore a suit of the dullest shade of taupe known to fashion. She'd pulled her shoulder-length hair into a low chignon and capped it off with a dark brown, feathered fascinator. If she'd been going for Duchess Kate chic, she missed the mark and hit Princess Anne doughty. Hard. She held out a gloved hand, presenting a small, red, velvet box. "I'd like to give you a wedding present from my family."

Jackie pried open the lid. Her breath caught. "It's magnificent." She turned the gift to show off the small circle of sapphires.

"It's an heirloom, belonging to the last Duchess of Effingham."

It had also adorned the gray suit Regina had worn upon her arrival the previous day.

Jackie turned to Diana. "Pin it on me. I'd like to wear it as my something-blue."

Diana did the honors, taking the opportunity to examine the broach as she fastened it to her mama's shoulder. Of the dozen karat-sized stones, the first ten in the circle were bright blue. However, the two taking up the eleven and twelve o'clock positions were darker.

Refracted the light differently. Appeared to her eye more valuable. Which were the replacements? Were the others real? Did Andrew know?

She pocketed the questions. While curiosity had certainly earned her the truth, it also paid dividends in pain. Besides, Mama liked the imitation pearls on her wrist as much as she did the genuine one in her ears.

"Looks like you're all set now. Grandmother Dansfield's pearl earrings are your something old, your dress is new, the bracelet is mine, and now you have something extra special as your blue."

Jackie dabbed at the corners of her eyes. "You've been so sweet to me, Regina."

This time Lady Somerset endured her hug with a little more grace. "I'm sure we're going to be great friends, Jackie." She turned to Diana. "I'd like for us to be friends as well."

The hairs on the back of her neck stood up. Images formed in her brain of a medieval knight sent as emissary from one feudal family to another. Exactly who had sent her into the Curtis stronghold? Neville? To have his sister surrender a piece of the Effingham jewels to the next duchess? Cecil? To further his matchmaking campaign? Andrew? To persuade her to listen to his explanation?

She smiled. "Bless your heart. Aren't you sweet. We were fixin' to leave for the church when you came by. You're welcome to ride with us if you like. The limo's got plenty of room for all of us."

"That's kind of you to offer." She gave the bling on Jackie's shoulder the same look as the barn cats did sparrows. "I wouldn't want to intrude. We can talk more at the reception."

After she left, Jackie walked over to examine herself in the mirror. "Glory be, it's pretty. Wonder if Neville's got any more of the family jewels back at his estate."

Diana stomach knotted. Alarm bells rang that weren't of the impending storm variety. Something wasn't quite on the up-and-up in the groom's family.

It's simply the reaffirmation you don't make the bridal cut in Andrew's book that has you out of sorts. Or maybe the weather.

She fished one of the antacids out of her bouquet. Crunching on the tablet, she took Mama by the elbow. "Perhaps that's a conversation for y'alls honeymoon." A clap of thunder sent a jolt through the whole room. "So much for that window of opportunity."

Jackie gave her reflection another look. "Rain is good luck on your wedding day."

Sequestered in the vicar's study, Andrew and his uncle bided their time. Reverend Beecham had already voiced his views on the sanctity of marriage, offered words of wisdom on the institution, and promised to collect them at the appointed time.

"Uncle, you're not wearing your signet ring." Andrew checked his watch, the last present he'd received from his father that Andrew didn't pay for.

Neville turned his hands over as if they belonged to someone else. "By jove, you're right. I left it on the dresser in my room."

"If we hurry, we can retrieve it in time for the ceremony. I think the rain has slacked off enough we won't drown."

"Rain or no. I'm not leaving this building until I'm a married man."

Andrew raised his hands in surrender. "All right. I was only checking."

"You can be assured of my steadfastness."

"I hope when my time comes, I can be equally certain of my decision." Except making up his mind wouldn't bring the desired outcome to fruition. If that were the case, he'd be rid of a pair of burdens and free to wed Diana.

The minister opened the door, cutting off his melancholy thoughts. "It's time, fellas. Chapel's full and the bride's a-waitin'."

Andrew followed behind the two older gentlemen, entering the church from a side door. Thankfully, the rain had slacked off so Pachelbel's "Canon in D" could be properly appreciated. The lovely melody filled the room as much as the scent from the gardenia's and roses did. Great swaths of white bunting lined the pews, and candles reflected light from the stained glass. Even the overcast sky added to the church's ambience rather than detracting from it. Diana knew how to organize a spectacular wedding—despite weather, time constraints, and the couple's myriad eccentricities.

Uncle Neville and Andrew took their places in front of the altar, cavalier and his second. One last matter before the bride came down the aisle. He turned his attention to the front row. His mother jerked her chin, indicating she'd complied with his not-so-subtle request to pass on the jewelry now Jackie's due.

The music changed to "The Wedding March," doors opened, and Andrew forgot about the terrific row he'd had with his mum that morning. He also forgot to breath. Diana floated down the aisle, blonde hair loose and cascading down her back, chin up, blue eyes sparkling—not meeting his.

"Unlock your knees," Uncle Neville muttered.

"What?"

"You're swaying, my boy. Unlock those knees of yours before you pass out."

Following his uncle's instructions did little to relieve the light-headedness. The page and bridesmaid entered, garnering a positive response from the wedding guests. The bride entered, smiling broadly. She passed her bouquet to Diana and joined hands with Neville. Still he couldn't quite manage to gather his wits.

Words like goddess and siren and angel came to mind. Except the heavenly body standing on the other side of her mother appeared more the fiery-sword-wielding variety than winged-harp-playing kind. He had a mountain of explaining to do following the nuptials.

Following an opening prayer and scripture reading, the minister addressed the congregation. "If there are any here who can give just cause why these two should not be joined in lawful matrimony, speak now or forever more hold your peace."

"I can."

A deep voice resonated through the chapel, echoing off the walls. Even the candles seem to respond, flickering wildly. A gasp rose up from the congregation. Every head swung to the man standing at the back of the church.

Ragged cowboy hat in hand. String tie around his neck. Long, dark hair pulled back in a ponytail.

Bile burned Andrew's throat.

The old pro from the casino.

The minister rapped the pulpit for silence. "What cause have you?"

"She's still married to me."

Daddy?

A wave of nausea washed over Diana no amount of antacid could soothe. Next to her, Mama gave a dramatic sigh and began listing to the right. Tossing the bouquets to the floor, Diana clambered for a shoulder. An arm. A hand. Jackie seemed destined for a hard landing until Andrew managed to put himself between her and the alter railing.

Diana patted Mama's hand. "Lord have mercy." The bride was in a dead faint. Figures the one at the center of all the drama would find a way to escape it. "Someone get her a glass of water." More hand patting and wedding program waving until Jasmine passed her a plastic bottle.

"Here you go."

Andrew lowered her to the floor. "Should we call nine-one-one?"

"Not yet. Let me see if I can bring her around." Diana poured a small quantity of water into her palm and used it to sprinkle her mama. "Wakey, wakey."

Jackie swatted at Diana and her reality baptism. "Stop, Diana. You're messing up my hairdo."

A roar from the back of the church got everyone's attention. Neville, Duke of Effingham, bastion of British aristocracy and good breeding, had removed his coat and engaged the interloper in fisticuffs.

Crack. Smack. Thud.

Fists met jaws, shoulders, soft middles.

"Andrew, Pastor Beecham," She waved wildly. Shock and horror played keep away with her heart. "Somebody stop them."

Good lord! People will talk about this day for generations to come.

Doc James and Wes Sr. beat Andrew there, separating the two combatants. Her favorite veterinarian held Dusty Curtis in a headlock, and Sergeant Doss escorted Neville back to the alter. The WWF entertainment over, the guests quieted as well.

Pastor Beecham cleared his throat. "Ladies and gentlemen,

under the circumstances, I believe it's best if we dismiss so we can give the families their privacy."

Diana's brain dropped the surreal in favor of the practical. "All that food." Chef had worked hours to present Jackie and Neville a wedding feast.

Andrew touched her arm. "May I offer a suggestion?"

Skip town?

Or he could give her a huge hug. She could stand for one of those right about now. Instead, she turned up her palms. "I'll take any help you've got."

"Send the guests to the church hall until your parents sort this out."

"Why didn't I think of that?"

"The biggest shock of your life, perhaps?"

She barked a laugh. "That'll do it."

"Ten minutes and I'm certain you'll have the problem managed."

"From your lips to God's ears."

"Would you like me to address the congregation?"

"Yeah. I'm not sure I could string that many words together."

"Ladies and gentlemen." His authoritative voice commanded attention. "Rather than leaving, please adjourn to the church hall. After we've celebrated for a while—"

And I retrieve Mama's divorce papers from the lockbox.

"—we'll reconvene for an uninterrupted ceremony."

Following his speech, he turned his attention to her. "Uncle Neville and I will return to the vicar's study and await word from you." His smile held more than a little sympathy. "Maybe this is a blessing in disguise your father has returned."

"After twenty years, I can't imagine that man's got much to say I want to hear."

She held on to Jackie, waiting for the chapel to empty, making a point of meeting the gazes of every derisive, arrogant, or condescending look shot their way.

I'll restore Mama's reputation.

She narrowed her focus on her so-called father.

Or kill someone trying.

With the gossips and voyeurs gone, Diana addressed the boot-clad elephant in the room. "First, you need to prove you're Dusty Curtis."

"He is." Jackie's voice came like the whimper of a kicked puppy. "A few wrinkles and gray hair haven't changed him that much."

"Fine. Then you stay put for a second while I go locate my mama's divorce papers."

"I'll save you some time, Diana Banana. There aren't any."

A memory flooded back. A piggyback ride through a cotton field. "Don't call me that. You forfeited the right to call me by anything but my given name a hundred skinned knees, two proms, and three graduations ago."

Dusty toed the floor. "I suppose you're right."

Diana turned to her mama, her anger not having been appeased in the least by her father's admission. "Please, for the love of all that's holy, tell me you got a divorce."

Jackie dabbed at the corners of her eyes and shrugged. "I assumed your granddaddy took care of it."

And why wouldn't she? Other than deciding to become a bigamist by marrying the duke, every important decision in Jackie's life had been undertaken by either her father or her daughter.

"You realize you came within a hair's breadth of breaking the law. You can't wish away a lawful marriage simply because it impedes a future one."

Jackie's sniffles returned. "I know I made a mess of things. What will everyone think?" She fanned her face. "They're probably all laughing at me. Jackie's not such a big shot now, is she. Not going to be marrying that duke after all." She let out a wail. "Oh my Lord, what's Neville going to do? He probably won't want me now."

Beyond the hurdles Diana and Andrew had created for Jackie and Neville and the trials of their own narcissistic inclinations, this last roadblock could prove the straw that broke the lovesick duke's back. "If Neville truly loves you, Mama, he'll wait while you get rid of this little legal hurdle."

Jackie sniffled. "You always know the right thing to say."

"Thank you, Mama." Diana guided her to the nearest pew. "Hang out here for a while. We'll go explain things to the Brits as soon as I have a word with *him*." She stormed the length of the chapel, coming head on with her father.

Dusty squared his shoulders. "I'm sure you must have a lot of questions for me, Diana. I'll answer anything you want."

"Not as many as you might think. I quit wondering things like where you were and why you didn't contact me back in the fifth grade."

He flinched. "I deserve that. I'll admit I haven't done much worth talking about, but you were never far from my thoughts. From what I've learned, you've become quite the successful business-woman. A chain of retail stores. Turned the old home place into a bed and breakfast. Bought the track of land off Highway 83."

"Who told you that?" Had he been keeping tabs on her all this time?

"The young man standing up with your mama's boyfriend. I believe he said his name was Andrew."

Pinpricks danced along her skin.

"Met him playing blackjack over at the Lucky Lady. Got to talking one night when the cards were being particularly unkind. He was going on about Greenbrier and these two women who own the place. And what a success it was."

Diana's palm itched to reacquaint itself with the viscount's cheek.

"I put two and two together and figured it was time to come collect what was mine."

Darn you, Andrew Montgomery!

Why the heck couldn't Andrew have been into golf or tennis like any other respectable rich guy? She was sure she could have found a polo pony for him to ride. Strangling him would have to keep. She had another man to set straight.

Diana tamped down the anger heating her breast, her neck, the tips of her ears. "I see how it is. Let me disabuse you of any notions you might have about common property. Jackie Dansfield Curtis owns *no-thing*. Not the car she drives. Not the garden she tends. Not the roof over her head. My granddaddy might have neglected to secure a divorce for his daughter, but he made certain she'd be well cared for by placing *eve-ry-thing* in my name."

He blinked.

"Don't bother saying you're hurt I would suggest you've come back solely for monetary reasons."

"You're not going to listen to my side of the story?"

"What side is that? The one where you took off with another woman, stayed away for two decades, and returned only when you thought there might be a payday in it." She pointed to the church doors. "When you make good use of those, be sure to leave your address with my friend who's waiting on the other side. We'll need it to serve you in the next day or two."

Dusty jerked a nod and turned on his heels. A brief exchange of words wafted in from the outside then silence.

For all the hear-me-roar she'd shown in the past few minutes, five-year-old Diana wanted to call her father back. She also wanted the man to be a better human being.

And to evade what came next. "No sense putting off the inevitable." She helped her mother to her feet. "What can't be cured, must be endured."

"Can you do the talking, sweetie? I don't even know where to begin?"

"Of course, Mama." Diana put her arm around her mama's waist. "Don't I always have your back? I'll put such a spin on this tragedy, Neville will see you as his damsel in distress, himself as Prince Charming, and your marriage to Daddy a dragon that needs slaying."

If that was the case, what role did she portray? Fairy godmother, needle-wielding-mouse, pumpkin?

And Andrew? Was he Diana's knight? If so, what color was his horse...white or black?

Diana despises me. I could see it in her eyes.

Andrew paced the vicar's study. She'd never believe he hadn't sought out Dusty. Never listen while he explained the conversation she'd overheard with his father. Never give him an opportunity to tell her how much he loved her.

He'd be lucky if she didn't give him a black eye to match his uncle's.

"You're wearing out the rug." The words came from a cut and bruised mouth. "Sit. Calm yourself." Neville gestured to a nearby chair. "The ladies will join us momentarily, and we'll go from there."

Despite the state of Neville's clothes and hair and the bruises forming on his face, the man remained as composed as he had prior to the ill-fated ceremony. "How can you be so—?"

A rap on the door had him rushing to open it. "Diana—"

The vicar's wife held up a towel-wrapped bundle. "I brought peas."

He blinked. "We're not hungry but thanks." He was beginning to grasp the southern penchant for feeding guests. Really…peas? Now?

She let out a breath. "They're frozen. I'm going to put them on the duke's face."

"You must think me daft. It's very good of you to think of him." Andrew attempted to accept the packet, only to have Mrs. Beecham hold them above her head.

She took a step across the threshold and craned her neck to see Neville. "Jackie is a friend of mine. I know she'd want me to take care of y'all."

Andrew blocked her path. "Thank you. I can see to him."

"Trying to lend a hand. It's the Christian thing to do."

"It's much appreciated." He took the offering, stepping forward so he could close the door. With her on the other side. "I'll be sure to mention this when we see her."

From the hallway she called, "Let me know if there is anything I can do."

"You're too kind."

Bloody hell, these were either the most gracious people on the planet. Or the nosiest.

Andrew passed the bag to Neville and took the seat next to him. "You look a frightful mess." His thoughts on Diana and how the revelation affected his chances with her had preempted the fact his uncle had been in a brawl.

"You should see the other guy." Neville chuckled. "Aw. That hurts." His face grew serious. "Worth it though. Embarrassing my Jackie."

"I'm sorry, Uncle, I should have insisted on seeing her divorce decree."

Neville patted Andrew's knee. "Not your responsibility." A smile replaced his stern expression. "Everything will work out. For all of us."

Does he know about Diana and me?

"Be patient and have faith in *our* women." He winked. "You'll see."

Having his secret known had a surprisingly uplifting effect. Air flowed more freely through his lungs. The knot in his belly uncoiled. His purpose redoubled. "You're right."

Knock, knock.

The weight returned.

Both their fates waited on the other side. He schooled his features. Willed calm. Pushed the nightmares to the far corners of his imagination.

"Open the door, my boy. Don't keep the ladies waiting."

Diana held onto her mama, her breath, and her courage. When Andrew opened the door to Reverend Beecham's study, they all escaped her grasp. He appeared calm. Emotionless. British reserve at its finest.

Jackie's stumble and whimper kept Diana focused on the mission at hand. She led her mama to the nearest chair, arranging her in the seat like a life-size doll. The duke took Jackie's hand, giving Diana the first glimmer of hope since her father's disastrous announcement.

"Tell us how it went, my dear." Neville brought Jackie's hand to his lips. "Shall we be returning to the chapel momentarily or in a few weeks' time?"

The duke's query acted like a fresh battery to an electronic toy. "Really?" Jackie fluffed her veil. Straightened her dress. "You still want me, Dukie Dear?"

He pouted, his bruised and swollen lip protruding further. "Have you so little faith in me? Of course, I still want you. Now, tell me, what's it to be?"

Her hands fluttered free from his. "Diana is so much better at explaining things than I am."

She drew in a breath. "It seems my father is correct. There is no divorce. However, given they haven't lived together in decades and share no property, I see no reason why a divorce can't be obtained in a matter of weeks."

Neville cocked an eyebrow. "An autumn wedding then."

"Perhaps you might consider a private affair this time." Andrew shook his head, a crack in his British reserve showing.

"Whatever Jackie wants." Neville tugged his fiancée to her feet. "Right now, we have guests to entertain."

Diana rubbed the pain in her middle. "I'll be with you in a moment, Mama. I want to freshen up." Too bad the church had a no-alcohol stance. She could use a belt of something strong before facing that crowd.

"You two take your time." Jackie hooked her arm through Neville's.

The duke leaned in and whispered loudly. "Maybe there'll be more than one announcement to make."

Diana's grasp on the situation snapped. Had Mama and Neville breezed over the pre-existing husband like it was a bigamy bump? Sailed off to a reception for a wedding that wasn't? Then inferred they knew she and Andrew were lovers? The furniture and books in the room swirled. She stumbled then reached out to steady herself. What next?

"Sit." Andrew led her to the chair Jackie vacated. "My mind's playing catch up as well."

"They know?"

"Appears so. Diana, you have to understand—"

She waved away his concern. Some issues were easy enough to work through. "You had no way of knowing. It was a complete accident, and considering the facts, a lucky thing for my mama."

He pulled the other chair so they sat knee-to-knee. "Was it a lucky thing for you though? Are you okay with seeing your father again?"

"I'm fine." She turned her head, so he couldn't see the welling tears. "My granddaddy was the perfect male role model for me. I was fine before Dusty popped back up, and I'll be fine, now."

Time to tackle the more difficult topics. Setting Andrew straight. Letting him go.

As her granddaddy always pointed out, the shortest distance between two points was a straight line. "Now I've got Mama settled, I'm going to take time off. Alone. Instead of Biloxi, I have a friend from Ole Miss who moved to Portland. I'm going pay her a visit. Who knows, maybe Oregon will suit me. I might stay."

"Please, hear me out." He took her hands.

Diana didn't have the will to pull from his grasp, but neither could she meet his gaze. She studied the moiré fabric of her dress and imagined the swirls and lines taking her far from this heartbreak. "If this is about the conversation with your father last night, I have a pretty good grasp of the situation. Your father wants you to marry me, and you don't want to."

"Not because I don't love you."

Her head popped up. "Say that again."

"Diana Frances Curtis. I. Love. You."

Those three words should have eased her pain. Should have

brought her joy. Should have made everything right. "It doesn't change anything though, does it? I'm not proper marriage material even if your father approves of me."

"He approves of your money."

When faced with losing his pride or losing Diana, it was no choice after all. "We're broke." Relief spread through him with the admission. "My uncle hasn't a *pence* to his name. Chatham Park is barely habitable. My parents *rent* their townhome in London. And the lot of them rely on me for their income. By gambling. I'm a professional. Over the years I've worked out a system that pays off rather reliably."

Diana pulled her hands from his. "You're a card shark."

"I count cards, which is perfectly legal." He banked on her family's history with the occupation and the emphasis she placed on a strong work ethic. "I've been at it consistently for years. I've avoided notice by keeping my winnings to small increments and moving around the globe. Not as glamourous as it sounds, but it pays the bills."

"That's what you've been doing?" Her eyes widened. "Not loafing? Working!"

"I have. My grand scheme was to make enough I could ask for this." He took her hand again, kissing her palm. "And only this. I never wanted you to think I was after your money."

She wiped away her tears. "Now look what you've done. I was all geared up to give you a piece of my mind."

"I'd settle for a piece of your heart."

"Are you proposing?" Her voice rose an octave.

"No. Not yet. Only once I've sufficiently proven I can support a wife on my own."

God, it could take years before he could accomplish such a feat.

She waggled her finger at him. "I'm still a little mad at you."

"I'm sure I've earned your ire."

"You should have told me all along. I don't care you and Neville aren't rich."

"You might not care, but I doubt very much we could have convinced you we weren't dishonest."

"It explains why you felt you had to marry someone from your social class. She would have brought an allowance or another fortune to the marriage."

"Or failing that, a woman of means—as my father was quick to point out." He tightened the grip on her hand. "That's truly the only reason I haven't already gotten down on bended knee."

Her small laugh gave him a glimmer of hope. "We've known each other, what, two weeks? And you feel you're late with the proposal."

"What can I say? My uncle and I know a good thing when we see it."

Diana's shoulders rose to her ears. "Where do we go from here?

We each have families to support. Careers that take us to different places."

Andrew pulled Diana from her seat. "Run away with me. Forget everything and everyone." He twirled her then caught her in his arms. "To start with, we'll visit your friend. When we need to replenish funds, we'll head to Vegas. I'll work, and you can lounge by the pool."

"You're crazy." She swatted his arm. "That's no way to live."

"Why not? I've been doing it since university. Now I'll have company. And inspiration."

"What about my businesses? Our families? You're saying we should cut them off?"

"Just until we have a better plan. Your shops are already well managed, and Jasmine is fully capable of running Greenbrier."

Diana tilted her chin. "Who'll run my mama?"

"It's time we both cut the apron strings, as it were. Neville and Jackie have each other now. I plan to have a conversation with my uncle regarding his renovation plans. His promises to Jackie regarding her new living quarters at Chatham Park will have to be revised." Andrew couldn't resist a taste of her lips. "I'll have more pressing matters to attend to than honoring *his* promises."

She didn't exactly pull away from his kisses. More on the order of offering other parts of her face while she continued with her questions. "And your parents? Aren't they also dependent on your income?"

"They are, but they're simply going to have to get jobs. Like the

rest of us."

So far, Diana approved of Andrew's line of thinking. Except for the part where she laid poolside while he did all the work. A seedling concept took root watered by fresh optimism and hope. "I have the perfect jobs for them."

"Just like that? You're brilliant as well as beautiful." He kissed the tip of her nose. "But I knew that from the moment I rescued you from the baggage carousel. Let's hear it."

"Your mother grew up at Chatham Park, right?"

"She did."

"And going by the rehearsal dinner, I gather your father is a wine aficionado."

"I'd call him a wine snob, but your way sounds nicer."

"Then let's put those skills to good use at Chatham Park. Lady Somerset can give guided tours and Lord Somerset can oversee wine tastings."

Her mind raced with possibilities. She loved conceptualizing new business schemes and playing an important role in helping Andrew made the prospects all the sweeter. "Beyond that, I'll study the market to see what's missing in the area. Wedding venue. Spa. Boutique Hotel. Luxury gardens. The avenues are endless. The economy is stronger now, so I don't see why your family home can't be as successful as mine. All it takes is time and an investment of capital."

"Sounds brilliant except for the last part. I've been working for years and can only keep our heads above water."

"That's why you need my money." She tapped her lips, mentally calculating which investments to pull from to get the cash. "I'm prepared to invest a minimum of a million. To start. It will likely take more, but that's enough to get the ball rolling. Architectural drawings, licenses and a proper business plan, then we'll see where we are."

"Hold up." Andrew took her by the shoulders, turning her face to meet his gaze. "This is exactly the argument I had with my father. Why I said I didn't want to marry you."

She narrowed her eyes at him. Enough was enough. "You have your damn pride."

"Look where it's gotten me." He kissed her light and quick. "I accept. I've had to manage things on my own for so long, I'm afraid I'm not very good at accepting help."

"We're both alike in that way. Cussedly independent."

"Bloody hell, can you imagine what our children will be like?"

Yes, I can. The heir, the spare, and the spare, spare.

"With your good looks and my sense of style, they'll be the beaus of every barbeque in Mississippi."

Andrew kissed her again, this time letting lingering, and through their touching lips he said, "or the belles of Britain."

EPILOGUE

Diana and Andrew didn't make it to Portland to visit her friend. Neither did they go to Las Vegas or even Biloxi. Instead, they spent the next six months at Greenbrier getting Mama divorced then *finally* married to Neville, handing over the B&B reins to Jasmine, and creating a plan for Chatham Park.

Unfortunately, they lost a year to a scheme that never quite got off the ground. Tea and Tours had fundamental issues. Every down-on-his-heels lord was running a tea shop out of his kitchen, so it was difficult to stand out. Also, as it turned out, they had personnel difficulties. Lord and Lady Somerset had a low tolerance for getting up before noon and patiently handling customers.

However, the second concept was the charm. On an especially rainy weekend, while Diana was inspecting Uncle Neville's extensive library, she discovered a number of old and rare manuscripts. She dug deeper and found more. While Effingham bank accounts might have been dwindling, it seemed the previous several dukes had a talent for collecting artifacts, small obscure paintings, and other literary works. An idea sparked, and thus the Duke of Effingham Center for Renaissance Research and Revival was born.

Hardly a weekend passed when the estate wasn't filled with academics and hobbyists paying handsomely for the privilege of viewing the collection or dressed in period costumes jousting, drinking mead, or recreating some aspect of the age.

Except for this weekend when Chatham Park was closed to the public for the marriage of Andrew David Neville Montgomery, Viscount Farthingworth, to Miss Diana Frances Curtis.

Wearing a ivory satin gown, Diana gazed out the window of her mama's suite of rooms. Rooms which had been beautifully, yet modestly, refurbished. The mid-June day was as free from rain as Mama's wedding days had had in abundance. A carriage and four white horses waited to take the bride to meet the man who held her heart.

The one who kept texting her every five minutes.

Did he think at this point I'm going to get cold feet?

She pressed her hand to her middle. Thanks to Andrew's steadfastness, she no longer needed a ready supply of antacids. No, a very wonderful surprise would join them in seven months. Diana could hardly wait to meet their little prince or princess.

"Quit daydreaming, girl. Time to shake a leg," Jasmine said. She and her family had made the trip across the pond. The new President of Greenbrier Enterprises would act as her matron of honor, while Master Sergeant Wesley Doss would accompany Diana down the church's aisle.

She tore herself from the view. "I was just wondering if the caterers had iced enough champagne." Not really. Diana was thinking of the weekend honeymoon to London. Two whole days completely alone with Andrew.

Mama fluttered over. "Let the staff worry about details." She held up her prized possession, one she'd wear every day if Neville hadn't convinced her otherwise. "Sit down so I can put this on you."

The hairdresser had already pinned a veil to the back of her chignon, so all that remained was for Mama to affix the Duchess of Effingham tiara. "Thanks for letting me borrow it, Mama."

Jackie beamed. "My pleasure, sugar. After all, it'll be yours someday."

"Not for a very, very long time, I hope, but I'm proud to wear it today." Not that it held much in the way of monetary value. The library wasn't the only thing Diana had inspected. That sapphire broach Andrew's mom gave Jackie: only two of the stones were real. The filigreed crown made of pearls and "diamonds": only the smallest stones had been left unpilfered.

Mama's happy little bubble didn't need pricking, and the long-ago swap didn't matter to Diana. She really was happy to join this respected and proud family.

With the tiara in place, Mama fluffed Diana's veil. A few tears shimmered in the duchess's eyes. "Are you ready, my dear?"

"Is Barbie's ass plastic?"

The women erupted in a fit of giggles. Just as she'd hoped. Mama wasn't the only one fighting the tears.

Jasmine wagged her finger at Diana. "You're going to have to give up your southern sayings when you become Andrew's viscountess."

"Never! He loves me just as I am."

That she knew to the bottom of her fancy new shoes, which held a brand new sixpence. An English wedding tradition. At the church, the combination of the stately stone and beautiful music brought solemnity and a sense of history to the day. And Wes Sr. handing her off with a kiss on the cheek did make her miss Granddaddy Dansfield.

Then Andrew took her hand, and all else faded away. "You are beautiful. I'm the luckiest man alive," he whispered in a voice thick with emotion.

The ornately robed vicar stepped forward. "Dearly Beloved…" He continued with his opening remarks while Diana's emotions bubbled just under the surface.

Love, joy, anticipation had her pulse racing.

"If any here can give just cause why these two should not be lawfully joined together in holy wedlock, speak now or forever hold your peace."

Andrew cut his eyes at her and winked.

She returned his smile.

The congregation remained silent.
No one would stop *this* wedding.

About the Author

Whether facing the demands of caring for a child with special needs or the struggles of a soldier returning home, Melissa Klein's characters take on the challenges life throws at them with perseverance, courage, and humor. Her favorite work-avoidance devices are gardening, reading, and playing with her grandsons. While she won Georgia Romance Writers Unpublished Maggie award in 2013 and Rose City Romance Writers Golden Rose award in 2012 she still hopes to win the lottery. If she does, she'll buy a huge farm in north Georgia and convince her children to live next door. Until that time, she lives in Atlanta with her husband, who puts up with frozen dinners with the words are flowing.

Melissa can be found at http://www.MelissaKleinRomance.com

More Books by Melissa Klein

A Risk Worth Taking

Her Hometown Hero

Blame It On The Snow

Theirs to Protect

Out of Bounds

Out of Sight

Out of Time

Love Around the Table

If You've Enjoyed this Book, Please Check Out These Other Titles from the Catalog of Rusty Wheels Media, LLC.

Quintessential Reality

Letters Never Meant to be Read (Volume II)

Letters Never Meant to be Read (Volume I)

Contractual Obligations

Worked Stiff: Poetry and Prose for the Common

Worked Stiff: Short Stories to Tell Your Boss

Where Did You Go?: A 21st Century Guide to Finding Yourself Again

The Forge: Certified Six Sigma Green Belt Certification Program Workbook

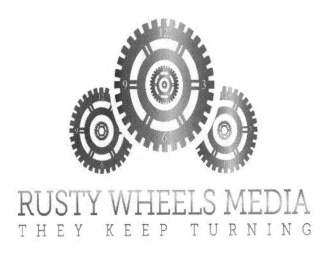

RUSTY WHEELS MEDIA
THEY KEEP TURNING

Made in the USA
Columbia, SC
23 February 2020